GOD'S
HEART
FOR YOU

GOD'S
HEART
FOR YOU
...Knowing His Love

CINDY DIFRANCO

ACW Press
Ozark, AL 36360

God's Heart for You
Copyright ©2004 Cindy DiFranco
All rights reserved

Cover Design by Alpha Advertising
Interior design by Pine Hill Graphics

Packaged by ACW Press
1200 Hwy 231 South #273
Ozark, AL 36360
www.acwpress.com
The views expressed or implied in this work do not necessarily reflect those of ACW Press. Ultimate design, content, and editorial accuracy of this work is the responsibility of the author(s).

Publisher's Cataloging-in-Publication Data
(Provided by Cassidy Cataloguing Services, Inc.)

DiFranco, Cindy.

   God's heart for you : -- knowing his love / Cindy diFranco. -- 1st. ed.
   --Eugene, Ore. : ACW Press, 2004

      p. ; cm.
      ISBN: 1-932124-27-6

   1. Christian life. 2. Spirituality. 3. Spiritual life. I. Title.

BV4501.3 .D54 2004
248.4--dc22   0402

Printed in the United States of America.

CONTENTS

I Love You!

*H*ave you ever had a best friend—someone you loved being with most of all? She was that person you enjoyed doing your favorite things with, the one you confided in and with whom you shared your most precious thoughts and dreams. She was also that person who loved being with you most of all.

I had a friend like that who I considered to be my best friend in all the world. We did everything together and truly trusted each other. We shared our dreams, our loves, and our disappointments. I'll never forget a particular day when I arrived at her apartment…in tears. I had just had a very rough day and was feeling so low and hurt inside. I just needed to be with my friend.

As she came out of her room to greet me, she saw the tears in my eyes and the expression of sadness on my face. Before I even had a chance to tell her what had happened to me, she started to cry! I had not even said a *word* to explain to her what my day had been like! Just by seeing how hurt I was, the tears came to her eyes. She really cared about me.

My best friend and I were really close and had spent a lot of time together. Although, it wasn't necessarily the amount of time that we spent together that made us so close. We can work with people all day but not be very close to them. My friend and I were close because we were open and shared our thoughts and deepest feelings with each other. We were close because we shared what was in our very hearts.

What about our relationship with God? How close and intimate is that relationship? Do we know each other really well? Do we know each other's thoughts and feelings? Does God know what is in our heart? Do we know what is in His heart?

One thing is very different when it comes to our relationship with God. When we enter into this relationship, He already knows everything there is to know about us—He knows our thoughts, desires, dreams, even how many hairs are on our heads! He also knows all that is in our hearts! The important piece that is missing is knowing *His heart*.

God *wants* us to know *His* heart: He wants us to know His love for us, what He thinks about us, the things that He desires for us to have, how He feels when we fail Him, and how He feels when we are walking close to Him. He desires an intimate relationship with each and every one of us that is deep and personal. God wants us to not just know *about* Him but to truly *know Him*!

When we enter into a relationship with God, it is like starting on a wonderful journey—a journey of growing to know Him and all that is in His heart. No matter how long we have been on this journey and no matter how many years we have been Christians, there is *always more* that He wants to show us about His heart!! The Bible says that His love for us is so great that it "surpasses knowledge!" Isn't it wonderful to know that we can learn so much about God's heart and His love for us and still there will always be *more*!

A few years ago, God gave me a *picture* in my mind to show me something that was in His heart. God will often do that to clarify

things He is trying to show me or teach me. This time it was a picture of Him. I could not clearly see Him and all that He looked like, but I knew it was God. I could sense His love, His tender compassion and the longing in His heart as He called out to everyone:

"I love you!"
"I LOVE YOU!!"
"I LOVE YOU!!!"

To my surprise, the people in this picture continued right on doing what they had been busy doing. It almost seemed as if they did not hear Him or could not hear Him. Amazingly, these people were not just those who did not know Him as Lord and Savior, but there were also many Christians. There was no response to His words of love. It was as if they had a deaf ear when it came to hearing Him say, "I love you."

This picture troubled me as I felt God's heart and His sadness. It left such a burden on my heart. Days later, God impressed upon me to "convey His heart to His people—with His heart." This book is one of the ways in which He has led me to do that. This book is actually a "love letter" to you from God. May He give me the right words to say so that His heart will actually reach through these pages...and touch your heart.

Why Is It So Important to Know God's Heart?

*C*an we truly trust someone if we don't believe that he loves us? Can we put our faith in someone if we don't believe that he sincerely cares about us? Even if someone truly loves us unconditionally, we will not be able to trust that person unless we believe that he loves us. We need to come to the point where we know this person's heart of love in order to place our faith in him.

The Bible says that "My righteous one will LIVE by faith" (Hebrews 10:38) and that "without faith, it is IMPOSSIBLE to please God" (Hebrews 11:6). Being able to put our faith in God is vitally important. In order for us to trust God and place our faith in Him, we need to understand His love for us. We need to know His heart of love for us personally.

The apostle Paul prayed a powerful prayer for the Christians in Ephesus that is God's desire for each one of us as well:

> *And I pray that out of His glorious riches He may*
> *strengthen you with power through His Spirit in your inner*

being, so that Christ may dwell in your hearts through faith. And I pray that you being ROOTED and ESTAB-LISHED in LOVE, may have power, together with all the saints, to grasp how WIDE and LONG and HIGH and DEEP is the LOVE OF CHRIST, and to KNOW THIS LOVE that SURPASSES KNOWLEDGE—that you may be FILLED to the MEASURE of ALL the FULL-NESS of GOD.

Ephesians 3:16-19

Paul knew the importance of knowing the love of God. He prayed for the Christians in Ephesus that they too would know His love that "surpasses knowledge." He prayed that each one of them would know how "wide, long, high and deep" the love of God was for them. He not only prayed that they would know how great God's love was for them, but that they would also "grasp" it. He wanted them to truly comprehend God's love for them, not just with their heads but with their hearts!

That is not just Paul's heart for the Christians in Ephesus, but it is also God's heart for all of us—for you and me. In order for us to be able to trust and put our faith in Him, we need to know His love!

BUILDING A FOUNDATION OF HIS LOVE

I am a parent of two lovely children. As I have enjoyed being their mom, the Lord has impressed upon me the importance of creating an environment of love for them to grow up in. I realize how important it is for their development and growth to have a foundation of unconditional love undergirding them. They need to be able to know, rest, and rely on my love for them. I may be disappointed at times about the *things* that they do wrong, but my love for *them* stays the same. They are always my dear children. I may discipline and correct them, but I do this in love. I try to make sure they know that I truly do love them and that I always will. When they encounter problems in their lives, I want them to know that they can come to me for help. I want them to know that they can always trust in my love for them.

That's the same way it is with God and His relationship with us. He wants us to be "rooted and established" in *His* love. Knowing His love is the foundation in our relationship with Him. Everything else is built on top of that!

Nobody would ever think about building a house without a strong foundation. If we did, the house would not stand very well during storms or strong winds. The foundation would not be strong enough to sustain the house. We would never build a house with a foundation of straw, mud, or twigs, for these things would never be able to hold it up. It would be wise to use something like bricks of cement or rock. As we built our house, we would not just use a few bricks but an abundance of strong bricks! The more bricks, the stronger the foundation and the better off our house would be.

Our relationship with God is similar. The more *bricks* of knowing His love, the stronger the foundation. How many *bricks* do you have in your foundation? How well do you know God's love? How many times have you come to a deeper knowledge of His great love for you personally? Get ready for some more *bricks*

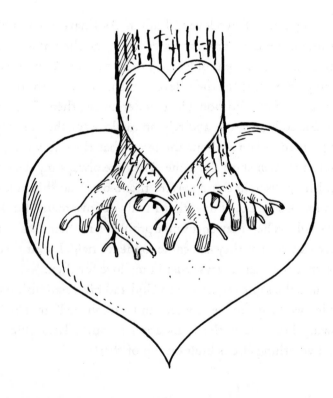

to come your way, for I believe that this is the reason God wanted me to write this book! (smile)

A few years ago, my sister agreed to let her four daughters hatch about a dozen baby chicks from eggs. (Brave sister!) A strong heat lamp was crucial for the eggs to be able to survive and hatch into cute little baby chicks. *Love is like our children's heat lamp*—our children will grow to their greatest potential as they grow in the *light of our love.*

We all need to grow in the *light of God's love.* To be able to mature to the fullest as Christians, we need to *grow in* the revelation of his love for us and also *grow up* in it. This will enable us to grow up to be the BEST that we can be in Christ!

We have all had different kinds of earthly fathers. Some were good and caring and others were probably not. God blessed me with a wonderful dad—I could not have asked for anyone better! He was always there for me, he always had a word of wisdom and advice, and he was always interested in everything that was happening in my life. I know that my dad loved me deeply. There were hard times in my life when I knew that if he could have, he would have taken my place and my sufferings and bore them for me. I know that he loved me that much!

Having a dad like that made it easier for me to understand and accept the love of my Heavenly Father. I am often in awe when I think that my dad was not perfect but God *is*, and that God's love for me is so much greater than anything I felt and experienced from my dad.

We can pray and ask God to help us to "know" His love, as Paul prayed for the Ephesians, no matter what kind of dad we have here. God wants us to "know" His love that "surpasses knowledge." He desires that we know His very heart for us!

No matter what storms come our way, He wants us to be anchored by His love. He wants us to "know and rely" on His "love for us" (1 John 4:16). He wants us to know that His love for us is our constant and our lifeline. It is the thing that will never change. His steadfast and unconditional love will always be there for us. He wants us to:

- KNOW His love,
- TRUST in His love,
- put our FAITH in His love, and
- GROW UP and MATURE inside His love so that we can be all that He called us to be.

MY CRUMBLING
FOUNDATION

*H*ave you ever had "one of those days," a day when everything seemed to go wrong? This was one of those days! I remember crying as I drove along, feeling so frustrated inside. I finally cried out to God and said, "It feels like my whole foundation of faith is crumbling away!" (What a mouthful!)

Immediately, I *heard* God say, "Good!" I said, "Good? How can that be good?" Then He gave me a *picture* in my mind of a foundation that was not built very well. I *saw* a foundation of many bricks: some stones looked good and strong, but many were old and crumbling. The mortar between the stones was cracked and not holding well. Then, to make things worse, I *saw* a big bulldozer coming along and plowing it all away so that there was nothing left!

I asked God, "What does this mean?" He showed me that during my years as a Christian, I had learned a lot of good things about Him that were correctly based on His Word. Unfortunately, I had also formulated some incorrect ideas about Him from false things I had heard and from wrong thinking. This made for a weak and unstable foundation. The *storm* had come that day and He showed me that my foundation was not strong enough to hold me up! My life had been built on a foundation that was a mess!

This picture really shook me up. I didn't know how to respond to what the Lord had shown me. Then He *told* me something that filled me with excitement! He *told* me that He was going to build a *new foundation of faith* in me! This time, He instructed me to build it *"brick by brick!"* He instructed me to not lay a *brick* down until I KNEW that it was "based on His Word and was true to His heart." He was going to build a foundation of faith in my life like I had never known before!

It's exciting to see how God has been doing that over these years. It was not until recently that I realized this foundation of faith was made up of *knowing His love for me*! The things He has taught me are all somehow related to how much He loves me. They are *bricks* of revelation that have caused this foundation to grow bigger and stronger...wider, longer, higher and deeper!

This deeper revelation of His love came in many ways and at various times in my life. It came during happy and blessed times. It also came during trials when He revealed His steadfast love for me and His power to get me through. Sometimes I would see and experience His love through people I met along the way. Very often, it would come simply through His Word and by His Holy Spirit who "teaches us all things" (John 14:26) and "guides us into all truth" (John 16:13).

No matter what way He chose to show and teach me about His love, it ultimately was backed by His Word. God's Word always needs to be the final authority for what we believe and put our faith in. What we learn always has to line up with His Word. *Brick by brick,* God has built a strong foundation of knowing His love that is true to His heart and based on His Word!

Even though my foundation is stronger than it ever was before, it is not fully complete. I do not know everything there is to know about God's heart and His love for me. I look forward to adding more *bricks* to my foundation in the years to come. It's exciting to know that there is always more that God desires to show us about His love that "surpasses knowledge." He *never* runs out!

From the Start— Just Wanting to Know His Heart

A few years ago, for a class at church, I was asked to write a paragraph about how I came to receive Jesus as my Lord and Savior. I was only thirteen when I went forward at an altar call. As I was thinking back to that day, I strained to remember what it was that prompted me to do that. I thought about the young man who came to our church that morning. He had brought his guitar with him and sang some beautiful songs about the Lord. He shared about Jesus, the Son of God, and how He loved us so much that He took our place on the cross and died so that we could be forgiven and have eternal life. He talked about the loving relationship he had with God and described it as being personal, intimate, and so fulfilling.

As I thought about that day, I remembered sitting there and thinking, "That's what I want in my life! I want to have a relationship like that! I want to know this God who loves me so much. I want to know Him like this man knows Him!" Yes, I did want to be forgiven for my sins and I did want to go to Heaven, but one of the main things I longed for was to know God's *love* like this man did. With tears in my eyes, I slid out of my pew and made my way to the front where I invited Jesus to come into my life as my Lord and Savior.

As I sat and wrote my paragraph about that day, I realized that from that time on, God had been *continually* revealing His love to me. I got excited as I thought how over these years, He had been showing me more and more of His very heart. He had been showing me His heart—right from the start.

God Loves Me?

*A*s I grew up and attended school, I never felt like I was anyone special. I was very quiet and shy and had only a few close friends who I spent time with. Nobody really noticed me during those years, and some days I felt as if I just blended into the wall. I knew that God was with me, but I did not have much revelation of how much He loved me. I felt as if I was nobody special that He would really care about me and the things I was dealing with in my life. However, I was *wrong* and God desperately wanted me to know how *special* I really was to Him.

After graduating from high school, I chose to attend a Christian college. I loved being there! It was wonderful to be surrounded by so many other Christians who loved God. One night, I sprained my ankle while playing basketball. I sprained it quite severely so that I could not bear weight on it without a great deal of pain. A friend of mine was nice enough to give me a piggyback ride back to the dormitory. Later that evening, some friends placed their hands on my ankle and prayed for it to be healed.

I remember sitting on the floor as they gathered around me to pray and thinking, "God, I know that You can heal my ankle! I've heard of You healing much bigger things than this!" That was my mentality as a young Christian, as if it really made a difference to God how big the problem was! (smile)

After they prayed, I got up to get back into my chair and put all my weight on my ankle, believing it to be fully healed. I almost fell into my chair face first because the pain was so awful! I felt quite embarrassed and somewhat discouraged. I sat there and tried to figure out why I didn't get healed, questioning my faith as well as my attitude, thinking that possibly I was lacking somewhere.

About thirty minutes passed and it was time to leave. As I stood up to go, I noticed that I had *no pain* in my ankle at all! It was completely pain-free! I remember stomping my foot on the floor as hard as I could in amazement and feeling such a surge of excitement! I was so elated that all I wanted to do was jog around the campus on my healed ankle and praise the Lord! So, that's what a friend of mine and I did that evening! It was great!

Nothing like this had ever happened to me before! I had heard about it happening to other people, but never to *me*! Even though being healed like this by the power of God was so wonderful, there was something that meant more to me than that. What touched my heart was the fact that God loved me so much that He cared about a little thing like a sprained ankle! I had not understood God's love for me as I had grown up, but that night, I *tasted* His love! God touched my heart even more than my ankle and helped me to realize how truly special I was to Him. He helped me to see a bit clearer that He loved me—He *really* loved me! He really loved me...ME!

GOD'S GREATEST EXPRESSION OF LOVE

*H*ealing my ankle was a beautiful expression of God's love for me. But, there is a verse in the Bible that talks about how God demonstrated His love for us to the *greatest* degree. I couldn't write this book without taking a moment to talk about this.

> *This is how God SHOWED HIS LOVE among us. He sent His one and only Son into the world that we might live through Him. This is love: not that we loved God, but that He loved us [you and me!] and sent His Son as an atoning sacrifice for our sins.*
>
> 1 John 4:9,10

Another verse talks about Jesus and says:

> *Having loved His own who were in the world, He now SHOWED them the FULL EXTENT of His LOVE.*
>
> John 13:1

God demonstrated His love for each one of us by giving us His Son Jesus. What does it mean that He was sent as an "atoning sacrifice for our sins"? It means that He took *our* place on the cross and died for *our* sins. Jesus never sinned in His entire life here on earth so He didn't deserve death. However, you and I have sinned, for the Bible says that "all have sinned" (Romans 3:23). It also says that the "wages of sin is death" (Romans 6:23). That means that *we* all deserved to die—not Jesus.

It's similar to a situation where someone was handed the death penalty and was scheduled to die, but a friend who loved him dearly offered to die in his place. It's also similar to a situation where someone had a large debt to pay and could never raise enough money to pay it but then a friend who loved him dearly offered to give everything he owned to pay it for him.

Jesus is like that friend. He gave everything He had in order to save us. He gave His very life. The Bible says, "Greater love has no man than this, that he lay down his life for his friends" (John 15:13). There truly is no greater love than His love for us! Jesus gave *everything* that He had to give—there was nothing more that He could have given. He left a beautiful Heaven to come here to die an agonizing death for us—for you and me.

If you or I were the only one alive on earth, He still would have come to die for us. I remember hearing that preached in a sermon once and it changed my life. To think that Jesus loves me *that* much! He loves each and everyone of us *that* much!

God did everything that there was to do to make a way for us to have a personal relationship with Him and to be able to go to Heaven. There's nothing left for us to do except receive what He already did!

It Is a Gift

For it is by GRACE you have been saved, through
FAITH—and this not from yourselves, it is the GIFT of
God—NOT BY WORKS, so that no one can boast.

Ephesians 2:9

A gift is something that we just receive. We don't pay for it, we don't work to earn it, we just open up our hands and receive it. In this case, we open up our hearts and our lives and receive Him!

> For God SO LOVED the world [with a love that "surpasses knowledge"] that He gave His One and Only Son, that WHOEVER believes in Him shall not perish but have eternal life.
>
> John 3:16

Jesus is God's most precious Gift to us. He is *the letter of Love* God sent to each one of us. He is the way God provided for us to be able to get to Him and He is the *only* way. If there were another way, then Jesus would have died in vain. He would have died for nothing. Jesus said:

> I am the way and the truth and the life. No one comes to the Father EXCEPT through Me.
>
> John 14:6

God sent His Son Jesus for each and everyone of us. The Bible says that God is "not wanting ANYONE to perish, but EVERYONE to come to repentance" (2 Peter 3:9). God loves us all the same and wants each one of us to accept His Son Jesus as his or her personal Lord and Savior.

HAVE YOU RECEIVED THIS GIFT?

God gives us all a free will, though, so He will never force anyone to do this. He has done everything necessary for us to have a relationship with Him and now He calls each one of us to come and receive what has already been done. He doesn't want even one to miss out on going to Heaven! He wants each one of us to have an intimate and close relationship with Him that will last for eternity!

If you have never prayed and asked Jesus to come into your life to be your Lord and Savior, then I humbly invite you to pray the following prayer or one that is similar. No other decision in our lives is more important than this one. This decision determines where we will be spending eternity. This decision determines if we will be forgiven and washed clean from all our sins—or carry them with us all the days of our lives. This decision determines whether or not we will have a personal relationship with God, our Creator—or go through our lives alone and without His presence and guidance each day. There is no better time to pray a prayer like this than right now. So if you have never done this, than please pray with me:

Dear Lord Jesus,
I know that I am a sinner and I need forgiveness. I believe that You are the Son of God and that You died on the cross for me. You paid the price for my sins in full. Please forgive me for all of my sins and wash me clean. I invite You into my life and into my heart to be my Lord and Savior. Fill me with Your Holy Spirit and lead me in my life. I want to live a life that is pleasing to You now.
Thank You, Lord. I believe that I have been forgiven and that You will never leave me. Now I know that I will indeed go to Heaven someday, where I will live with You for eternity!
In Jesus' name, Amen.

A New Creation!

If you just said that prayer, then I am so excited for you! The Bible says that you have been forgiven and washed clean from all of your sins and that you are actually a "new creation"!

Therefore, if anyone is in Christ, he is a NEW CREATION; the old has gone, the new has come!

2 Corinthians 5:17

Yet to all who received Him, to those who believed in His name, He gave the right to become CHILDREN OF GOD—children born not of natural descent, nor of human decision or a husband's will, but BORN OF GOD.

John 1:12,13

"The word is near you; it is in your mouth and in your heart," that is, the word of faith we are proclaiming: That if you confess with your mouth, "Jesus is Lord," and believe in your heart that God raised Him from the dead, YOU WILL BE SAVED.

Romans 10:9

The Bible also refers to you as one of His "dearly loved children" (Ephesians 5:1), "heirs of God and co-heirs with Christ" (Romans 8:17), and "the righteousness of God!" (2 Corinthians 5:21). You have His Spirit (Romans 8:9) and so Christ actually lives in you! (Galatians 2:20). You do not have to depend just on your own strength and wisdom, but now you have all of His within you to rest and rely on. For He promises that He "will never leave you; never will He forsake you" (Hebrews 13:5).

Never again will you have to wonder *if* you will go to Heaven someday. God promises that you *will* and wants you to *know* this and never question it ever again:

I write these things to you who believe in the name of the Son of God so that you may KNOW THAT YOU HAVE ETERNAL LIFE!

1 John 5:13

Oh, and there is so much more! As you read His Word on your own, you will see all that He desires for you and all of the promises that are yours as a child of God. As you place your faith in Him and in His Word for you, you will find that having a relationship with God is the most wonderful and exciting experience of your life!

GOD LOVES ME
AS MUCH AS JESUS?

*J*esus is the Son of God, so we know that *He* is God's Son. He never sinned and always did what was right. We can see how He *deserves* to be called the Son of God. However, God calls you and me His "dearly loved children" as well! (Ephesians 5:1). Even though we are not perfect and still fall into sin, God calls *us* His sons and daughters!

> *I will be a Father to YOU, and YOU will be My SONS*
> *and DAUGHTERS, says the Lord Almighty.*
>
> 2 Corinthians 6:18

> *For you did not receive a spirit that makes you a slave*
> *again to fear, but you received the Spirit of SONSHIP. And*
> *by Him we cry, "Abba, Father." The Spirit himself testifies*
> *with our spirit that we are GOD'S CHILDREN.*
>
> Romans 8:15,16

The word *Abba* means "father" or "daddy." It is an endearing name to call someone who is a loving parent to you—a parent who you feel close to. Jesus used the word *Abba* when He prayed in the Garden of Gethsemane. God is His "Abba" and He is also *our* "Abba"!

We are not only God's sons and daughters along with Jesus, but God also loves *us* as much as He loves *Him*! If you're anything like me, you are probably thinking, "How can that be true? I am not perfect like Jesus. How can God love me as much as He loves Jesus?" Let's look at what the Word of God says about this:

Jesus prayed in the garden: "May THEY [you and me!] be brought to complete unity to let the world know that You sent Me and have LOVED THEM [you and me!] EVEN AS YOU HAVE LOVED ME!

John 17:23

There it is, right in God's Word! Jesus was thinking and praying for us in the garden right before He went to the cross! God loves us so much and wants us to know that He loves us with the *same love* that He has for Jesus! Now that is a *big brick!* (smile)

Seeing His Heart
through
My Little Girl

As I was working at the computer one day, trying to get some work done, my daughter ran in, all excited. She breezed in with something urgent to her at the moment. I was a little frustrated and feeling as if I was already behind schedule in what I had hoped to get accomplished. I barely looked up and answered her question as quickly as I could so that I could return to my project. She quietly continued to stand there, looking for more from me than that short answer.

I finally turned around and gave her my full attention. As I looked into her big brown eyes, I heard God say, "I wish I could look into her eyes like that and have her look into My eyes. I wish I could physically lift her up and hold her in My lap." The tears welled up in my eyes as I got a glimpse of God's heart and His desire to be able to have a close relationship with us and how, in a way, (for lack of a better word) He *envies* us. How God longs to be *close* to us, to *hold* and *embrace* us, to *talk* with us and *listen* to us talk with Him, and to not only *look* into *our* eyes, but have *us look* into *His eyes*.

Looking into someone's eyes, is the closest thing to looking into someone's heart. There is no other place to look at a person to get a better glimpse of that person's heart. What will it be like when we get to Heaven and can actually look into the eyes of Jesus? I imagine that His eyes will be full of the purest of love, so sincere and so deep. His eyes will radiate the tender love He has in His heart for me. I know that as I look into them, that love will touch and penetrate my heart like never before.

I can't wait to look into the eyes of the One who has this love for me that far exceeds any love I have ever known. And you know what? I know that He is looking forward to that day as well—He is looking forward to the day when *together* we can look into one another's eyes!

Not Just
"One of the Crowd"

As I was thinking about God's love for me one day, I began to question how He could love all of us with so much love. I started to think that because there were *so many* Christians in the world, I must not be very important to Him. Really, how could we all be so special to Him when there are so many of us to have a relationship with? I started to feel as if I were just "one of the crowd." I had the misconception that God must just love us all, like a big *lump* of people!

Then God helped me understand how He really feels about each one of us. He had me look at my favorite relationship, which is the one I had with my best friend. He had me think about how I felt toward her and how involved I was in her life. He had me think about the way I loved her and how close we were. He impressed upon me that this is how He feels towards *me* but to an even greater and deeper degree! He showed me that He is God and, because He is omnipotent, He is able to look and be involved with me as if I were:

HIS FAVORITE!

He looked at me and worked on our relationship:

AS IF I WERE THE ONLY ONE!

Suddenly, I felt so special to know that God loved me like that and cared about everything in my life! I realized that God not only cared about everything in my life but wanted to be totally involved in every aspect of it as well! Psalm 139 beautifully shows us God's heart concerning this:

O Lord, You have searched me
and You know me.
You know when I sit and when I rise;
You perceive my thoughts from afar.
You discern my going out and my lying down;
You are familiar with all my ways.
Before a word is on my tongue
You know it completely, O Lord.

You hem me in—behind and before;
You have laid Your hand upon me.
Such knowledge is too wonderful for me,
Too lofty for me to attain.

Where can I go from Your Spirit?
Where can I flee from Your presence?
If I go up to the Heavens, You are there;
If I make my bed in the depths, you are there.
If I rise on the wings of the dawn,
If I settle on the far side of the sea,
Even there Your hand will guide me,
Your right hand will hold me fast.

If I say, "Surely the darkness will hide me
And the light become night around me,"
Even the darkness will not be dark to You;
The night will shine like the day,
For darkness is as light to You.

For You created my inmost being;
You knit me together in my mother's womb.
I praise You because I am fearfully
And wonderfully made;
Your works are wonderful,
I know that full well.
My frame was not hidden from You
When I was made in the secret place.
When I was woven together in the
Depths of the earth,
Your eyes saw my unformed body.
All the days ordained for me
Were written in Your book
Before one of them came to be.

How precious to me are Your
Thoughts, O God!
How vast is the sum of them!
Were I to count them,
They would outnumber the grains of sand.
When I awake,
I am still with You.

Psalm 139:1-18

God is omnipotent, which means that He is able to be everywhere at all times! This enables Him to have a relationship with each and every one of us as if we were the only one on earth! We, on the other hand, are only able to divide our time and interests to accommodate a handful of people in our lives, but God is *God!* He is able to focus and love each and every one of us intimately, just as it describes in this psalm.

How many times do we think about God each day? Well, He is *constantly* thinking about each of us—all day! Do we know what He is doing? Well, He *always* knows what we are doing! Do we know what He is thinking? Well, He *always* knows exactly what is on our minds! He is familiar with *all* of our ways, *all* of the time! God is awesome, not just because He is *able* to do that in each one of our lives, but because He *desires* to do that in each one of our lives!

GOD IS FOR US—
100 PERCENT FOR US!

I used to have the misconception that God is like someone playing a big chess game in our lives. However, I used to see Him playing on *both* sides of the game. I saw Him moving the pieces that were *for* me—but then I would also see Him as moving the pieces *against* me. I thought He was not only moving pieces to bless me, but also to bring calamities into my life!

God showed me that He is only playing on one side of the chess game—our side. He is always in our corner and "for us." He is not making bad things happen in our lives but rather working to give us the strength to overcome them when they do happen! The Bible says:

> *If God is FOR us who can be AGAINST us? He who did not spare His own Son, but gave Him up for us all—how will He not also, along with Him, GRACIOUSLY GIVE US ALL THINGS?*
>
> Romans 8:31,32

God showed me that when the Bible says that He is "for us," it doesn't mean that He is only 50 percent for us, or 75 percent for us or 99.9 percent for us, but rather He is 100 percent for us—100 percent of the time!

The Bible says:

> The Lord is GOOD TO ALL; He has compassion on ALL He has made.
> The Lord is faithful to all His promises and LOVING toward ALL He has made.
> The Lord is righteous in all His ways and LOVING toward ALL He has made.
>
> Psalm 145:9,13,17

God's heart is always desiring "good" for us:

> "For I know the plans I have for you," declares the Lord, "plans to PROSPER you and NOT TO HARM you, plans to give you a HOPE AND A FUTURE."
>
> Jeremiah 29:11

> Don't be deceived my brothers. Every GOOD AND PERFECT GIFT is from above, coming down from the FATHER OF THE HEAVENLY LIGHTS, who does not change like shifting shadows.
>
> James 1:16,17

> Taste and see that the Lord is GOOD; BLESSED is the man who takes refuge in Him.
>
> Psalm 34:8

God is good, good, ...so good! There is nobody better at being good! You could say that He is the "goodest" of all!

There is nobody else who loves us as God does! His love is "perfect" (1 John 4:18). I used to read the chapter about love

(1 Corinthians 13) and feel as if it were only telling me how I should love other people. I always felt as if I came up short and I did not love to the degree that these verses described love.

Then God showed me that He was not just describing how *we* should love other people, but He was also describing how *He* loved US! His love is like the love described in this chapter, for how could He ever expect us to love to a greater degree than He does! In fact, we cannot truly love as this chapter encourages us to love, unless we know His love first!

> *Love is patient, love is kind. It does not envy, it does not boast, it is not proud. It is not rude, it is not self-seeking, it is not easily angered, it keeps no record of wrongs. Love does not delight in evil but rejoices with the truth. It always protects, always trusts, always hopes, always perseveres.*
>
> *Love never fails. But where there are prophesies, they will cease; where there are tongues, they will be stilled; where there is knowledge, it will pass away...And now these three remain: faith, hope and love. But the greatest of these is love.*
>
> 1 Corinthians 13:4-8, 13

God's love for us is so great that the Bible even says that "God IS love" (1 John 16). That doesn't mean that God is just some emotion, but rather that LOVE is so characteristic of Him that this is the only way that they could describe Him! His love is so great that it "*always* protects, *always* trusts, *always* hopes and *always* perseveres!" He is 100 percent "for us"—*always*! ...And nothing "will be able to separate us from the love of God that is in Christ Jesus our Lord" (Romans 8:39).

"In All Things God Works for the Good"

*A*s I was praying one day, I *heard* God say:

"My people are abusing My Word!"

He referred me to Romans 8:28 which states:

And we know that in all things God works for the good of those who love Him, who have been called according to His purpose.

He went on to show me that many of His people were standing on this verse of Scripture and *embracing* the things that the enemy was doing to them instead of "resisting" him.

These people were of course trying to be *good Christians* and were doing this with a *good* heart toward God, thinking that these bad things were in some way *from* Him. They had the misconception that everything that happened in their lives was automatically from God—so they embraced these things.

What does this verse *really* say? It says that God is able to make everything "work" for the "good." It does not say that God *makes* or *causes* everything to happen in our lives. It does not say that everything that happens in our lives is from Him. He says that He is able to take everything that happens to us and make it "work" out for our "good"! He can do this AS we pray and put our faith in Him to do this.

There is another verse which has also confused people at times:

Be joyful always; pray continually, give thanks in all cir-
cumstances, for this is God's will for you in Christ Jesus.
1 Thessalonians 5:16-18

I used to have the misconception that this verse was saying that "all circumstances" were God's will for me. However, that is not what this verse says. It says that I am to be thankful "IN all circumstances." God is saying that despite whatever is happening in my life, He wants me to maintain a thankful heart toward Him. The verse is saying that He wants me to always be joyful, always pray and always be thankful in all circumstances. God wants us to be thankful all the time!

It is not God who causes the bad things to happen in our lives but He is able to take even the bad things and *turn them around* to make them "work" for our "good"! He can take what the enemy intended for evil and turn it around and bring good out of it. We can be thankful in knowing that God will do this AS we put our faith in Him.

A good example of this is the story about Joseph, who had been thrown into a pit and then sold into slavery by his brothers. His brothers had been very jealous of him and hated him. Joseph went through many ordeals because of what his brothers did in sinning against him but finally ended up with the Pharaoh putting him in charge of all of Egypt. Then he was able to save the people, including his own family, from a great famine! At the end, Joseph made a powerful statement to his brothers. He said, "YOU intended to harm me, BUT GOD intended it for GOOD to accomplish what is now being done, the saving of many lives" (Genesis 50:20).

God "worked" for "good" in what happened to Joseph. It was *not* His will for Joseph's brothers to throw him into a pit and sell him into slavery. If we said that this was God's will, we would be saying that it was God's will for his brothers to sin, because what they did was sin. It is never the will of God for people to sin! No, God "worked" in Joseph's life and took what the enemy meant for evil and brought "good" out of it! He is such an awesome God!

God Wants Us to Resist the Enemy!

Not everything that happens in our lives is necessarily from God. That has been a misconception at times. The Bible clearly states that we have an enemy and we are to "resist" him when he tries to do evil to us, not *embrace* the things that he tries to do to us. The Bible tells us to:

> Resist him [Satan], standing firm in the faith, because you know that your brothers throughout the world are undergoing the same kind of sufferings.
>
> 1 Peter 5:9

God also tells us to "put on the full armor of God!" He warns us of the enemy and tells *us* to do something about him! If everything that happened in our lives was orchestrated by God, there would be no need to wear "armor" and no need to "resist." The Bible says:

> Finally, be strong in the Lord and in His mighty power. Put on the full armor of God so that you can take your stand

against the devil's schemes. For our struggle is not against
flesh and blood, but against the rulers, against the authori-
ties, against the powers of this dark world and against the
spiritual forces of evil in the heavenly realms. Therefore put
on the full armor of God, so that when the day of evil
comes, you may be able to stand your ground, and after you
have done everything, to stand.

Ephesians 6:10-13

God is emphatically reminding us that we have an enemy
who comes to "steal, to kill and to destroy" us (John 10:10). God
is telling us to do something when evil comes—not sit back and
accept these things as being part of God's plan for our lives. God
is saying to "do everything" to oppose the enemy!

In order for us to do that, we first need to know God's heart
regarding the situations in our lives. We can discover His heart
by reading His Word to find out what things He loves and what
things He hates. We can see how God's plan for us is good: "'For
I know the plans I have for you,' declares the Lord, 'plans to pros-
per you and not to harm you, plans to give you a hope and a
future'" (Jeremiah 29:11).

We also need to know what things the enemy wants to do in
our lives. Jesus said that the enemy comes to "steal, to kill, and to
destroy." One of the first things God spoke to me as I was growing in my relationship with Him was, "No compromise—this is
not a game!" He was telling me that I had an enemy who was out
to try to steal from me, destroy me, and even kill me! He was
encouraging me to walk with Him and stay close to Him so that
I would not give the enemy an opportunity to hurt me. God not
only wants me to not give the enemy an opportunity, but also to
resist him.

Jesus is always our best example. We can read how He resis-
ted the enemy as He walked upon the earth. We can also read
how He came "to DESTROY the devil's work" (1 John 3:8). Jesus

hated the things that the enemy did to people and He went around *undoing* those things. When people were sick, He healed them, when people were in bondage, He delivered them, when people didn't have enough, He provided for them, and when people were deceived into believing the enemy's lies, He freed them by telling them the Truth! The things He did were completely the *opposite* of what the enemy did! Jesus said that He came "that we may have LIFE, and have it to the FULL!"

God showed me that a general way of knowing what is of Him and what is of the enemy is just to make two columns with each of these headings at the top. The things that tried to "steal, kill and destroy" me were from the enemy, and the things that brought me fullness in my life or abundance were from Him. That helped me a lot.

That is not to say that Satan cannot tempt us with good things to get us off track. He tried to do that to Jesus in the wilderness. However, for the most part, God is behind the "good gifts" (James 1:16) and Satan is behind the things that bring destruction.

Once we find out what is of the enemy, we need to take our stand against him as the Word of God says! God talks about putting on the full armor of God and tells us to "take up the shield of faith, with which to EXTINGUISH ALL THE FLAMING ARROWS OF THE EVIL ONE." Those arrows are the things that the enemy is shooting at us. God showed me that if we *embrace* those things that the enemy throws at us, it is as if we are catching the arrows and piercing ourselves with them! Sounds a little gory but God clearly got the point across to me! (smile!) We are to "resist" the enemy and *everything* that he throws at us! We are to "resist him, standing firm in the faith"!

WE ARE MORE THAN CONQUERORS!

Each time I read those verses, I imagine someone who is standing his ground! He is not giving up his land and all that belongs to him "in Christ." He is not moving, not giving an inch, not budging! He *knows* the heart of God and all that God wants for his life! He *knows* the covenant he has with his Heavenly Father through the blood of Jesus Christ! I can envision someone who is standing in victory with a winning flag in his hand, someone who knows God's heart for him and is standing to either keep it or get it back—someone who is standing as "MORE THAN A CONQUEROR" (Romans 8:37).

If we are called to "resist" the enemy and to put on the "full armor of God," then what are our chances of winning this battle? Do we have the power to do this? YES! We can be thankful because the Word of God tells us clearly that we have *more* power than the enemy does! Satan is just a fallen angel and he is a defeated foe! We never have to be afraid of the enemy. Jesus said,

> *I have given you authority to trample on snakes and scorpions and to OVERCOME ALL THE POWER OF THE ENEMY; NOTHING WILL HARM YOU.*
>
> Luke 10:19

> *You dear children, are from God and have overcome them, because the One who is IN you, is GREATER than the one who is in the world.*
>
> 1 John 4:4

> *Submit yourselves then to God. RESIST the devil, and he will FLEE from you.*
>
> James 4:7

We "resist" and "overcome" the enemy with the Word of God, which is our "sword." We can read how Jesus used God's Word three times when He was in the desert! It was very effective in defeating the enemy. He is our best example. We can also use the name of Jesus and the power of the blood of the Lamb as weapons against him. Also we have the powerful Holy Spirit living within us. God's heart is that we resist the enemy and all that he would try to do to us, which is why He has given us all we need to defeat him and has made us to be "MORE THAN CONQUERORS"!

Does God Really Allow bad Things to Happen to Us?

If I had a friend who was nice to me one day and then mean to me the next, I would not trust her very much and would probably not want to be with her. If I found out that she was spending time with someone who wanted to hurt me and planning with that person to do something bad to me, I probably would cease to be her friend. Most people would feel like that. They would look at this person as being two-faced, hypocritical, and not a friend at all! So, why do many people accuse God of doing these things to them all of the time and then for some reason justify this as being right? Why is that? If God would be displeased with us for acting like that to someone, then why would He want us to say that *He* is that way?

As God began to reveal His heart to me, He showed me how grieved He was with things I would say about Him. I had learned that God did not *cause* bad things to happen to me, but I would often use the statement that He *allowed* these bad things to happen to me.

God showed me that when I used the word *allow* to describe something bad that happened in my life, it was really just a *nice* way of saying that it was His will for that bad thing to happen to me. I felt His grief that day and I realized I had hurt Him by saying such things that were not true to His heart. He showed me that it made Him look like a God who purposely took three steps backward to *let* Satan do something harmful to one of His children. It also made Him look like a hypocrite, Someone who would be seen in His Word as one way, but *purposely* want the opposite to happen in our lives. So, I made a promise to Him to never again use the word *allow* in this way. I knew that everything in His Word pointed to the fact that He is a "good" God, desiring only *good* for His "dearly loved children."

GOD LOVES US MORE THAN WE LOVE OUR OWN CHILDREN

One day the Lord showed me the severity of thinking God purposely allows bad things to happen to us. A terrible report on the news told about a couple who was accused of intentionally letting their little child starve to death, and also accused of being responsible for the death of another child. I remember listening to the news and feeling utterly repulsed at the thought of a parent *purposely* sitting back and *letting* their child die from starvation. With children of my own, I could not even imagine how anyone could do such a terrible thing!

Then God *said*, "That is how many people talk about Me all the time." He explained that they look at Him as just sitting back and *allowing* His children to suffer and possibly die. I'm sure most people were repulsed when they heard the news that day. Most people could not imagine how parents could purposely injure their children or *allow* them to suffer! So, why are we not repulsed to think about God in this way? If we love our children so much that we could not even imagine hurting them in any way, then how can we think that God's love would be any less than that?

God's love for *His* children is greater than our love for *our* children. I thought about how I feel when my children are sick, or when they have had a bad day at school, or when they have done poorly during a sports game, or when friends have said things to hurt them. I *ache* for them and with them. Many times I have hurt so much that I wished I could take their pain and bear it myself! If they hurt, I hurt; if they feel pain, I feel pain; if they are sad, I am sad. I love them so much. God loves us *even more* than we love our children and when we hurt, He hurts as well!

BAD THINGS COME FROM A BAD ENEMY

So where do bad things come from? Unfortunately, we live in a world where we do have an enemy who is out to "kill, steal, and destroy" us. We can *see* his handiwork all around us! When bad things happen to us, *He* is in some way behind it and gloating over it.

A number of things give the enemy a foothold in our lives. Sin is one of the biggest ways in which the enemy is able to harm people. It began with Adam and Eve and it is still true today. Sin opens the door for the enemy and makes us vulnerable to him.

God has given us each a free will, so He will let us sin and go our own way. God never forces us to obey Him. He did not force Adam and Eve and He does not force us. He *wants* us to obey Him and lets us know that it is always beneficial for us to do so. God *wants* us safe and protected, and being obedient actually helps to keep us safe!

I will never say that God purposely *allows* bad things to happen to us, but He does *allow* us to sin, to not follow Him, to not pray and seek His will for our lives, to not read His Word, etc., and those things may bring about some bad consequences. He will *allow* us to make a mess of our lives and go in the wrong direction if that is what we want to do. He *allows* what *we allow* because He has given us a free will. We can read in the Bible how this is true—over and over again, people sinned and it led to some kind of misfortune every time.

Even during those times, what is God's heart toward us? Even if our own sin gets us into a mess, His heart is *always* full of love for us. He hurts and aches when He sees us suffering from the consequences of our own sin. His desire is to deliver us from those bad consequences, and He is able to do that when we ask Him to forgive us and repent of that sin. His love is steadfast, so it doesn't change! It is unconditional, so His love always stays the same, whether we are living in sin or living for Him!

Sin is just one of the things that give the enemy an open door in our lives. No matter how the enemy gets a hold in our lives, God is always "for us" and desiring to deliver us from all the trouble he brings. God is not just sitting back and *allowing* the enemy to do bad things to us, but He is very busy doing what He can to help us to overcome him!

WHAT IS
THE TRUTH ABOUT
GOD'S SOVEREIGNTY?

*H*ave you ever heard people say, "God is in control"? It could pertain to something good that had just occurred or something that was bad. Maybe you have heard someone say, "Everything that happens, happens for a reason," when he has just gone through a difficult time. As I listened to people try to explain why things happened, I found that many of them talked as if God were in control of the whole world. Many people seemed to think that everything that happened here on earth was somehow orchestrated by God—all the good and all the bad!

As I discovered more about God's heart, I saw a problem with this. I saw many evil things in the world: deaths, accidents, racism, stealing, rapes, etc. Many of them were sinful and all were destructive in some way. I knew that they were not of God. As I sought Him for answers, He also taught me more about His heart.

First, He showed me what the Bible had to say about Satan and, unfortunately, about his authority:

Satan is "the RULER of the kingdom of the air,"
Ephesians 2:2

Satan is "the PRINCE of this world," John 12:31,
14:30, 16:11

"The whole world is UNDER THE CONTROL of
the evil one." 1 John 5:19

It wasn't what I wanted to hear, but it explained a lot, especially when it came to all of the evil things that I saw happening in the world. It certainly made it clear that God was not in *control* of everything, nor was He to blame for all of the bad things I saw happening each day! I wish it wasn't that way. I wish God *was* in control of everything! Think about what a great world it would be!

Even though it is clear that Satan has some control and power here, the Bible is clear that he does not have authority or dominion over us as Christians. Jesus said:

I have given YOU authority to trample on snakes and scorpions and to OVERCOME ALL THE POWER OF THE ENEMY; nothing will harm you.

Luke 10:19

Submit yourselves, then to God. Resist the devil, and he will FLEE FROM YOU.

James 4:7

So, even though the Bible clearly says that Satan has some power, as Christians we need to realize that Jesus gave *us* authority over him! We need to do more than just know about this— we need to use that authority!

IT STARTED WITH ADAM

How did Satan get to be the "prince of this world" and the "ruler of the kingdom of the air"? I knew that God did not intend for him to have so much authority. God showed me that unfortunately, it was man who caused this to happen. ADAM bowed his knee to Satan in the Garden of Eden by obeying him rather than God. In Genesis, we can read how God gave "dominion" or authority over everything on earth to man! God's intention was for man to have dominion here—not Satan. Satan is referred to as just a fallen angel. After Adam disobeyed God by eating of the tree of the knowledge of good and evil and obeyed Satan instead, Satan was given this authority. God gave Adam a "lease" over the earth, and Adam unfortunately handed it over to the enemy!

> *Therefore, just as sin entered the world through ONE MAN, and DEATH through SIN, and in this way death came to ALL MEN, because all sinned—for before the law was given, sin was in the world. But sin is not taken into account when there is no law. Nevertheless, death reigned from the time of Adam to the time of Moses, even over those who did not sin by breaking a command, as did Adam, who was a pattern of the One to come.*
>
> Romans 5:12-14

God helped me to understand that when He created man, He created him with a free will and so therefore, he had a free will to either obey or disobey God. Adam chose to sin and because of his sin, "death came to all men." Then we were all born into sin and therefore, into death. It was mankind's fault that Satan was given so much authority here. Unfortunately, man opened the door for sin and for Satan here in this world.

When God first created man, there was no sin and Satan did not have any control. God made a beautiful and sinless earth where there was no sickness, pain, suffering, or lack. He made it that way because it was His will for it to be that way! He made it that way *for us*. Then the result of sin and Satan dramatically changed everything! All of the beauty and the perfection that God created for us out of His great love started to deteriorate because of man's sin and the work of Satan.

GOD LIMITED HIMSELF

So, what does sovereign really mean? It doesn't mean that God is in control of the entire world, because we can read in His Word that unfortunately "the world is under the control of the evil one." So, what does this mean?

About two weeks after I started to seriously pray about this, God *spoke* to me. It was not an audible voice but it was so loud that it seemed like one! I *heard* Him say:

"I am sovereign. I am sovereign and in My sovereignty,
I chose to limit Myself, out of My love for you!!"

Initially, I did not understand it. I just sat there thinking about what God had said. As I did, He showed me that when He gave man a free will, He limited Himself. When He created man with a free will, He relinquished his control over them to make them do what He wanted them to do.

With that free will came the consequences of those choices. The consequences of how we use our free will can either be good or bad. The Bible clearly tells us that if we follow after His Spirit, it will lead to life, but if we follow our sinful nature, it will lead to some kind of death in our lives (Romans 8:5-14). I could see in the Bible how God was able to bless His people when they followed and obeyed Him, but it led to disaster if they chose to follow sin.

What was His purpose in limiting Himself like this? Why did God choose to create us this way? He showed me that He did this because He loved us! What I *heard* Him say that day was:

"I chose to do this because I longed to have true sons and daughters…I longed to have true sons and daughters who would love Me just because they chose to love Me. I wanted true sons and daughters who would obey Me just because they loved Me. I wanted true sons and daughters who would serve Me just because they loved Me."

God wanted a family of sons and daughters—sons and daughters who would choose Him out of their own free will! In the Word of God, we read:

> As God has said: "I will live with them and walk among them, and I will be their God, and they will be My people…I will be a Father to you, and you will be My sons and daughters, says the Lord Almighty."
>
> 2 Corinthians 6:16,18

When Jesus rose from the grave, He told Mary, "Do not hold on to Me, for I have not yet returned to the Father. Go instead to My brothers and tell them, 'I am returning to My Father and YOUR Father, to My God and YOUR God" (John 20:17).

God helped me to realize that He could have created us like robots, programmed to obey Him and do whatever He wanted. He is sovereign and so He could have created us any way He wanted to! Out of His sovereignty, He chose to create us this way. God desired a family who would choose to love Him and obey Him out of their own free will.

Think about what it would have been like if He had not created us in this way. We would have been no more than robots or slaves with no freedom to choose what we wanted. We would have not been individuals, free to develop and grow as we willed. We would have been programmed to do God's will without a choice of our own.

LIMITED BY HIS WORD

One way that God limited Himself was by giving us a free will. Then He went a step further to limit Himself by speaking out His Word. God is limited by His own Word! If He speaks something out, it *has* to come to pass! God set down spiritual laws in His Word that have to happen because He said that they would. Why? It's because God cannot lie! He is a perfect God who is without sin. God is a holy God and everything He says is the Truth and has to come to pass. He limited Himself by His own Word, which is something that He cannot go back on. He cannot nor will He ever turn from His Word! God says:

> *I will not violate My covenant or alter what My lips have uttered.*
>
> Psalm 89:34

> *God did this so that, by two unchangeable things in which it is IMPOSSIBLE FOR GOD TO LIE, we who have fled to take hold of the hope offered to us may be greatly encouraged.*
>
> Hebrews 6:18

God stands behind His Word. We can trust that what He says is true—for God cannot lie. God is bound by His own Word. Praise God that it is this way! Therefore, we can have no doubt of His Word! We can put our faith in it and stand on it! God's Word is always true for each one of us.

LIMITED BY HIS HOLINESS

God is a loving God but He is also a holy God. He is also limited by the fact that He is holy. God needs us to be holy in order for Him to have a relationship with us. God *wants* to have a close relationship with each and every one of us but He cannot have a close relationship with someone who is not holy. We can read stories in the Bible how people who were not holy foolishly came into the presence of God and, because of their own sin, were destroyed. God's holiness and sin do not go together—if they come in contact with each other, there is an *explosion!*

Jesus came to fix this problem. When we accept Him as our Lord and Savior, our sins are forgiven and we are *made* holy (1 Peter 2:9). Then God is able to do what He desires most, which is to have a close, intimate, and personal relationship with each and every one of us!

God is limited by at least three things here:

1. The fact that He gave us a free will,
2. The fact that He cannot lie and is therefore bound by His Word,
3. The fact that He is a holy God and therefore needs us to be holy in order to have a close, intimate relationship with Him.

So, God truly IS sovereign! God chose to create man in this way; it was His choice! He was able to do everything He did in the ways that He did it. Why? Because He is sovereign!

Lɪᴍɪᴛɪɴɢ Hɪᴍꜱᴇʟꜰ Oᴜᴛ ᴏꜰ Hɪꜱ Lᴏᴠᴇ ꜰᴏʀ Uꜱ

As I prayed about this, God continued to show me the depth of His heart. I thought about His sovereignty and how the Almighty God, Creator of Heaven and Earth had limited Himself. I thought about all He had done in order to have true sons and daughters like you and me. He went through so much to have children whom He could have an intimate relationship with—children He could love as His very own and who would willingly love Him back as their Father.

I thought of so many stories about couples who wanted to have or adopt a child of their own. Some had paid large sums of money to adopt a baby. Some had even traveled to foreign countries to get a child of their own. Some had spent thousands of dollars and much of their time on new fertilization techniques. Some had even hired surrogate mothers to bear children for them.

As I thought about all of these stories, I realized that even though these couples gave so much, they only gave a *fraction* in comparison to all God gave to be able to have us! God went through so much more so that He could have children!

First, God made the choice to limit Himself when He gave us our own free will. As our Creator, He gave up that control over us, which was rightfully His, to allow us to make our own decisions. He was hurt when Adam sinned, and that sin not only caused a wall between Him and the children He loved, but it also opened the door for the enemy to come in and cause destruction. Although He made us "in His image" to be holy, He was grieved again and again by our choices to sin and therefore be unholy.

Then, God sent His prophets to tell us about who He was, and that He needed us to be holy. He sent us His law to show us what sin was and when He did, He helped us to realize that we needed a Savior. He also sent His Word to teach us more about Himself, how we should live, and to proclaim that a Savior was coming.

Then finally, He sent His only Son to be that Savior, to die on a cross for our sins to give us the way back to Him! God gave *everything* that He had to give! Why? Everything that God did was in order to have true sons and daughters. His purpose for doing all of this was to have children who would freely love Him—He did it so that He could have *us*!

DOES GOD CONTROL OUR LIVES?

As a physical therapist, I've heard many of my patients use expressions like, "God never gives us more than we can handle," when they talked about their illnesses. They would imply that God was in control of everything that happened in their lives, and that included all the bad things as well as the good.

I wondered about this as I heard many of my Christian friends use the expression that "God was in control of everything that happened in their lives." I knew that God was not in control of the world, but what about my life as a Christian? I knew that there were times and events that God was in control of, such as the rapture, the second coming of Christ, Christ's thousand-year reign on earth, Satan's final end in the lake of fire, etc., but what about my life? After I asked Jesus to come into my life and be my Lord and Savior, did everything that happened to me occur because it was His will? Was He in absolute control of my life?

God answered that question in part when He told me about Romans 8:28. I knew that there was an enemy in the world who was out to "kill, to steal and to destroy" me. God had impressed upon me the importance of "resisting" the enemy and putting on the "full armor of God" to take my "stand" against him. I knew what would happen to me if I chose to not do that and to *embrace* the things that the enemy threw at me. With that, I knew that God was not in control of everything that was happening in my life and that I had a vital part to play in how my life went.

How does the enemy get in there to do these things to us in the first place? I knew that Jesus gave *us* authority over the enemy and that we had more power than he had. It is God's will that we are always protected and safe from the enemy. Satan is not just our enemy, but also God's enemy as well. God showed me several things that unfortunately can make us vulnerable to him:

SIN

In your anger do not sin: Do not let the sun go down while
you are still angry, and do not give the devil a FOOTHOLD.
Ephesians 4:26,27

What is a *foothold?* The King James Version says, "give no place to the devil" and the Revised Standard Version uses the word *opportunity.* All imply that we open the door for the enemy when we sin by holding onto our anger. Unfortunately, we can see in the Bible that we open the door for the enemy when we sin in *any way.*

God gave me a *picture* to teach me what it was like. He showed me how He is our fortress and our refuge as it says in Psalm 91:

He who dwells in the shelter of the Most High will rest in the
shadow of the Almighty. I will say of the Lord, "He is my
REFUGE and my FORTRESS, my God, in whom I trust."
Psalm 91:1,2

If you make the Most High your dwelling—even the Lord,
who is my REFUGE—then NO HARM will befall you,
NO DISASTER will come near your tent.
Psalm 91:9,10

This is a beautiful psalm about God's protection for us. We are safe as we "dwell" in Him, as we "abide" (John 15:7; KJV) in Him and as we "walk in His Spirit," (Galatians 5:16; KJV) or rather as we stay *close* to Him in *obedience*. However, when we choose to sin, it is like foolishly going outside the safe walls of the fortress—outside where there are *dragons* that can harm us. Outside His fortress, the enemy can hurt us.

We can read how Jesus walked through angry crowds of people and escaped harm. Nobody could harm Him until He willingly laid down His life. He made this profound statement, "No one takes it from Me, but I lay it down of My own accord" (John 10:18). Jesus is the perfect example and He lived in safety because He was abiding in the Father and did not sin. The enemy could not touch Him.

Sin can cause us to reap destruction in our lives:

Do not be deceived: God cannot be mocked. A man
REAPS WHAT HE SOWS. The one who sows to please
his SINFUL NATURE will from that nature reap
DESTRUCTION. The one who sows to please the
SPIRIT will from the Spirit reap ETERNAL LIFE.

Galatians 6:7,8

Sin makes us vulnerable to the enemy and can bring destruction to our lives but it can also limit God from working in our lives.

How oft did they provoke Him in the wilderness, and
grieve Him in the desert! Yea, they turned back and
tempted God, and LIMITED the Holy One of Israel.

Psalm 78:40,41

God loves us so much and He desires to give us abundant life and good gifts. However, when we sin, God is often *unable* to do all that He wants to do in our lives. It creates a wall between God and us and hurts our fellowship with Him.

God doesn't put up this wall—rather, *we* put it up. He can't take the wall down either. *We* have to do that through asking God to forgive us and repenting of our sins.

> *Do not let this Book of the Law depart from your mouth; meditate on it day and night, so that you may be careful to DO EVERYTHING written in it. THEN you will be PROSPEROUS and SUCCESSFUL.*
>
> Joshua 1:8

Sin is a major thing that can make us vulnerable to the enemy. God warns us over and over again in His Word to not sin, for our own good! He is being a good Father to us. Just as our earthly fathers say, "Don't play in the busy street," and "Don't play with matches," because these things will hurt us, God is saying, "Don't go out of the safe walls of My fortress! He says with a tender heart, "I love you! Please, don't go out there!"

IGNORANCE

My people are destroyed from LACK OF KNOWLEDGE.

Hosea 4:6

This verse is talking about God's "people." God is saying that His people perish because they do not know His Word, which is where we get our knowledge and learn His Truth. That is where we learn about all the promises He has for us, who He is, His very heart for us, and who we are "in Christ."

Without knowing the Word of God, we have nothing concrete to put our faith in or to stand on. The Word of God "builds us up" and "gives us an inheritance" (Acts 20:32).

> *All scripture is GOD-BREATHED and is useful for teaching, rebuking, correcting and training in righteousness, so that the man of God may be THOROUGHLY EQUIPPED for EVERY GOOD WORK.*
>
> 2 Timothy 3:16,17

God's Word equips us thoroughly and without it, we are vulnerable to the enemy. It is His Truth for each one of us and nothing can come against it! God's Word will stand for *eternity!*

> *For you have been born again, not of perishable seed, but of imperishable, through the living and enduring WORD OF GOD. For, "All men are like grass, and all their glory is like the flowers of the field; the grass withers and the flowers fall, but the WORD OF THE LORD STANDS FOREVER!"*
>
> 1 Peter 1:23-25

In Ephesians 6:13-17, God tells us to put on the full armor of God. It's amazing to see that this armor of protection for us is made up of knowing God's Word! Knowing His Word keeps us safe!!

- Belt of "Truth"—God's Truth is found in His *Word!*
- Breastplate of "Righteousness"—knowing our right-standing with God is found in His *Word!*
- "Gospel" of Peace—the gospel is found in His *Word!*
- Shield of "Faith"—The two things that we place our faith in are God and His *Word!*
- Helmet of "Salvation"—His *Word* is what tells us about our salvation!
- Sword of the Spirit—which IS the *Word* of God!

The Word of God makes up the bulk of our armor in all of these ways! It is powerful to know and to use against the enemy.

> *As the rain and the snow come down from heaven, and do not return to it without watering the earth and making it bud and flourish, so that it yields seed for the sower and bread for the eater, so is MY WORD that goes out from My mouth: It will NOT return to Me empty, but WILL*

ACCOMPLISH what I DESIRE and ACHIEVE the
PURPOSE for which I sent it.

Isaiah 55:10,11

The Bible also talks about the great power that is in the Word of God when it says:

For the WORD OF GOD is LIVING AND ACTIVE.
Sharper than any double-edged sword, it penetrates even to
dividing soul and spirit, joints and marrow; it judges the
thoughts and attitudes of the heart.

Hebrews 4:12

We need to "renew our minds" so that we won't "conform any longer to the pattern of this world." This will enable us to "be able to test and approve what God's will is—His good, pleasing and perfect will"! (Romans 12:2). The best way to renew our minds is by reading God's Word! In fact, God tells us to "let the Word of God DWELL in us RICHLY" (Colossians 3:16). It also says that "Man does not LIVE on bread alone, but on EVERY WORD that comes from the mouth of God" (Matthew 4:4). The "Word is a lamp to my feet and a light for my path" (Psalm 119:105).

We need to take time to read God's Word. No other book is more important. We can never say, "I just don't have time or I am too busy to read this." God said that "My people are destroyed from lack of knowledge." In other words, our lives actually depend on how much we know of His Word! It is vitally important for us to read His Word and to know His Word in our hearts!

FEAR

Fear is the opposite of faith. Fear is believing the lies of the enemy and putting our faith in what he says, instead of what

God says. All through the Bible, God tells us, or rather commands us, to "not fear"! Fear is another thing that opens the door for the enemy in our lives.

> For God did not give us a SPIRIT of timidity [or fear], but
> a spirit of POWER, of LOVE and of SELF-DISCIPLINE
> (or a sound mind).
>
> 2 Timothy 1:7

Fear is not of God but rather of the enemy. If the enemy attacks us with fear, it is so important to deal with the fear and get rid of it first. Then we will be able to stand by faith in God and in His Word.

> There is NO FEAR IN LOVE. But PERFECT LOVE
> drives out FEAR, because fear has to do with punishment.
> The one who fears is not made perfect in love.
>
> 1 John 4:16-18

The Lord showed me that as I know His love and His very heart for me, there will be no room or place for fear to get in. As I come to realize His great love for me, *I will not fear*. I know that He is faithful to take care of me, provide for me, guide me, and protect me. Why? It's because He loves me! He is the Almighty God and He is "for me" 100 percent of the time!

> The Lord is my light and my salvation—whom shall I
> fear? The Lord is the stronghold of my life—of whom shall
> I be afraid?!
>
> Psalm 27:1

> Even though I walk through the valley of death, I will
> FEAR NO EVIL, for You are with me; Your rod and Your
> staff, they comfort me.
>
> Psalm 23:4

Lack of Faith

He [Jesus] could not do any miracles there, except lay His hands on a few sick people and heal them. And He was amazed at their LACK OF FAITH.

Mark 6:4-6

Jesus *could not* do the things that He had done in the other towns, because of their lack of faith. Our lack of faith can also limit God in our lives.

In the Bible we read how the Hebrews wandered around in the wilderness for forty years and were unable to enter the Promised Land during this time. Why?

So we see that they were not able to enter, because of their UNBELIEF.

Hebrews 3:19

Unforgiveness

But if you do not forgive men their sins, your Father will not forgive your sins.

Matthew 6:12-15

That is such a strong statement. The sin of unforgiveness is great and builds a wall not only between two people, but also between God and people. It limits God greatly in our lives to the point where He is unable to forgive us for our sins. God *wants* to forgive us for all of our sins. He sent His Son Jesus to die on a cross so that He would be able to forgive us! Unfortunately, when we hold onto unforgiveness in our hearts, it prevents God from forgiving us.

Prayerlessness

The Bible says:

You do not have, because you do not ask God.

James 4:2

So many people do not have the things that God desires to give them because they do not ask Him. This can be due to being too busy to spend time praying or maybe there are other reasons. Some people may feel as if they are bothering God and feel that they are in some way being thoughtful to not take up His time with their requests. God's heart *aches* for us to talk with Him and to ask Him for what we need and want. God wants to hear all that is in our hearts and on our minds. He wants us to pray about everything! The Bible actually tells us to "pray without ceasing" (1 Thessalonians 5:17 KJV). I guess it is safe to assume that God never gets tired of hearing us. (smile) He wants to spend not just a portion of the day with us, but *all day*. He is limited by our not praying and asking Him for the things we need in our lives.

Prayer connects us to the Living God in conversation. It's our twenty-four-hour-a-day *free* phone line to God! There's never a busy signal, there's never a recorded message telling you to leave your name and number and He will call you back, and there's never a time when He cannot be reached because He is out of town! He is always available to talk with us any hour of any day, and we can talk with Him anywhere!

Prayer is not just talking to God but also listening to Him talk to us. He will tell us which way to go and what to do by His Holy Spirit living within us; we will be "led by the Spirit of God" (Romans 8:14). The Bible says:

> *My sheep LISTEN to My voice; I know them, and they follow Me.*
>
> John 10:27

> *If any of you lacks wisdom, he should ask God, who gives generously to all without finding fault, and it WILL be given to him.*
>
> James 1:5

Negative Words

What we say with our mouths does indeed affect our lives, either for good or evil. In Genesis, we can read how God created the world by speaking words out of His mouth. He simply said, "Let there be light," and there was light!! He is a God of faith and when He speaks things out of His mouth, THEY COME TO BE!

The Bible says that we are made in the "image of God" (Genesis 1:27). He has also created us with power in our tongues that can be used for good or evil.

The tongue has the power of life and death.

Proverbs 18:21

For by your words, you will be acquitted, and by your words you will be condemned.

Matthew 12:37

God wants us to speak out the good things that He wants for our lives. In the book of James, God teaches us a lot about the power of the tongue:

We all stumble in many ways. If anyone is never at fault in what he says, he is a perfect man, able to keep his whole body in check.

When we put bits into the mouths of horses to make them obey us, we can TURN the whole animal. Or take ships as an example. Although they are so large and are driven by strong winds, they are STEERED by a very small rudder wherever the pilot wants to go. Likewise the tongue is a small part of the body, but it makes great boasts. Consider what a great forest is SET ON FIRE by a small spark. The tongue also is a fire, a world of evil among the parts of the body. It corrupts the whole person, SETS THE WHOLE COURSE OF HIS LIFE on fire, and is itself set on fire by hell.

James 3:2-6

That verse means that if we say a lot of negative words, we will experience negative things happening in our lives. Many people go around professing doom and gloom and being very pessimistic about their lives. They may say things like, "I always get sick during the winter," or "I always lose my luggage when I go on a trip," or "Everyone in my family got cancer so I guess I will get it too," or "I can never remember things," or "I think I am going crazy," or "Everyone who gets old gets aches and pains," etc.! What are you saying with your mouth? So often, we don't think about what we are really saying. If we only knew the power of those words and how those negative words "steer" our lives, we would change them in a minute!

I used to say a lot of negative things without realizing the effect it was having on my life. I now try to be more aware of what I am saying each day. Instead of my tongue "setting the whole course of my life on fire," I use it to "steer" my life into the will of God by saying things that line up with His Word and the wonderful things that He wants for my life. In fact, we cannot go wrong when we speak out His Word each day.

PSYCHIC PHENOMENA

Unfortunately, dabbling in the psychic realm has grown quite popular these days. Many people go into it lightly, as if there is nothing wrong with this. Many are just curious and they do not realize that they are in dangerous territory! It's like touching a flame of fire. It's not a question of maybe getting burned, it is a guarantee that you will get burned!

This can range from the psychic hotline, getting your fortune told, palm reading, tarot cards, Ouija boards, eight balls, astronomical signs, etc. These are things that we need to avoid as Christians. They are spiritual things that tend to grab people's attention and curiosity, but they are spiritually of the enemy and *not of God!*

The enemy can tell you things that have happened in your life because he knows them. This is not hard for him to do. He can also possibly figure out in what direction your life is going, although he does not know the future as our God does. If he can tell you something to keep you coming back for more, he will do it and try to lead you in the wrong direction. What is his purpose? It is to "steal, to kill, and to destroy," as usual!

Getting involved in things like this opens the door for the enemy. These things belong to the occult, no matter how nice or friendly these people appear. We do not want to be walking *toward* the enemy, but rather *away* from him! I have heard of numerous incidents where people naively got involved in these things and paid a high price for it, ranging from constant nightmares to sickness, to emotional disorders, to fears, etc. It took God's power to deliver them from these things that the enemy put on them.

It is not the power of God that equips a fortune teller in telling your future. If it is not God, then we should want no part of it. God wants us to turn to Him for direction and guidance. He is more than able to do that in our lives. There is nobody better to guide us and give us wisdom, since He alone knows all things!

GENERATIONAL CURSES

There are such things as curses and bondages, which are a result of sin, that can be passed down from one generation to another. I think that it is more than a coincidence that families often are more prone to certain diseases, bondages, sins, character traits, etc.

> You shall not make for yourself an idol in the form of anything in heaven above or on the earth beneath or in the waters below. You shall not bow down to them or worship them; for I, the Lord your God, punishing the children for

the sin of the fathers to the third and fourth generation of
those who hate Me, but showing love to a thousand genera-
tions of those who love Me and keep My commandments.

Exodus 20:4-6

This is stated several times in the Bible. The Word of God shows us how detrimental sin is to our lives and even to our families, even from one generation to the next! Where is the heart of God in this? Does God want to punish people? Does He want the sin of some to negatively affect the lives of those who will be born after them? Of course not! That is not God's heart at all. God says this in His Word to *warn* us of the result of sin! It is a spiritual law that the result of sin is death and destruction, which can affect not only us but generations after us! God grieves when He sees the awful result of sin! He is crying out like any father, saying, "Please do not sin—don't go there!"

In God's power we can find and receive deliverance from such things. The power of the blood of Jesus is so strong that it can overcome any and all generational curses! God sent a way of deliverance from generational curses by sending His Son as an atonement for not just our sins, but also the sins of the generations before us and after us!

God has shown me some things that can open the door for the enemy in our lives. I know that there are others still. An unthankful heart can limit God as well as wrong motives. Unfortunately, not everything that happens in our lives is orchestrated by God—but often by the enemy if we find these loopholes in our lives.

MAKING JESUS TRULY LORD

For weeks, I thought about these things that God had shown me. As I was walking down the aisle of the grocery store one day, I *heard* Him express how much He wanted to be in control. What He desires in each of our lives is that we walk closely to Him, "abiding" in Him and "walking in His Spirit" so that *everything that does happen in our lives is from Him!*

What God told me is that He cannot be in control of anything that He is not Lord over. As we give Him Lordship of our lives, then and only then can He be in control and bring about the good things that He desires for us! Many times He has shown me areas of my life that I had not truly made Him Lord over. Even though I *thought* I had, I was unfortunately being lord over these things instead of Him. He was therefore unable to work in those areas as He wanted to and unable to bless them as He desired. As we walk with Him and make Him truly Lord, then He can be in control and be Lord over those things in our lives.

Where is God completely in control? He is in control of Heaven! He is Lord there and everything that is done is according to His will. What is Heaven like? There is no sickness, no sin, no poverty or lack, no profanity, no hatred, etc. Heaven is that way because it is God's will that it be like that! Since He is in control there, His will is done! What God wants is to bring the things that are in Heaven to Earth! That is the reason that He asks us to pray that His "will be done on earth AS it is in Heaven" (Matthew 6:10). He asks us to pray that because it is His will that it be done, not just in our lives as Christians, but over all of the earth!

I thought, "Lord, how do I do this? How do I stay so close to you that I am always protected, and Your will is always being done in my life?" I was reminded of all of the things that could possibly open the door for the enemy. I thought: "I need to be obedient, I need to know Your Word, I need to use my faith and not give in to fear, I need to walk in love and not in unforgiveness, I need to have a thankful heart, I need to have pure motives and I need to stay close to You in prayer." This looked like such a tall order! I wondered how I could ever do all of this.

The Lord quieted my heart and said that all that is required is simply seeking Him first in my life. As I have a heart that loves Him and makes Him truly Lord in my life, these other things will fall into place. As I seek Him first, I will do the things that I need to do to stay close to God. The Bible says:

> Seek first His kingdom and His righteousness and all these things will be given to you as well.
>
> Matthew 6:33

God wants to be in control of our lives but not like some dominating dictator. Rather, He wants to be a Father to us and have us follow Him out of our love for Him. As we seek Him first in our lives, we give Him Lordship and then He is able to guide us, teach us, bless us, protect us, and bring about His perfect will for our lives.

How Should We
Look at Trials?

*H*ave you ever gone through a trial and been tempted to question why and even to question God's love for you? I have been there and done that.

Now I have a different perspective since God has taught me more about His heart and His love for me. I know that His love for me "surpasses knowledge" and that He didn't *allow* these bad things to happen to me. I know that I am His child and no matter what comes my way, He is 100 percent "for me" and always with me to get me through trials with victory!

God's love is my foundation and I need to be "rooted and established" in it all the time, but *especially* when I face trials. If I am not, it will be like standing on shaky ground. Think about someone who is trying to climb a mountain. He needs to have a sure footing for each step to make a successful climb. Being rooted in the love of God and knowing beyond a shadow of a doubt that He loves us perfectly is our *sure footing* when going through trials.

God does not send terrible trials into my life. Trials come because of the world I live in. They come from sin and the result of sin that is here. Trials come because I have an enemy who comes to "kill, steal and destroy." Those things that fall under the heading of killing, stealing, and destroying are from the enemy. On the other hand, the things that fall under the heading of "good" and "abundant life" are from God!

The Bible makes it clear that God is on OUR side:

> *If anyone does attack you, it WILL NOT BE MY DOING!*
> Isaiah 54:15

One night, I attended a church service where people gave their testimonies. Each one told about a trial or calamity in his or her life. They shared how God got them through the trial, but something just did not seem right as I listened to them talk. They often said that God *allowed* these bad things and that it was His will that these things happened. Many of these trials ended with terrible results that hurt both them and their families.

I left there with an awful feeling inside. I left there feeling as if God were someone who not only wanted us to go through trials, but also someone who just hovered over us to see how we were going to handle them! It made me feel as if God was someone who was distant and unfeeling and who caused trials to come our way just for the sake of testing us.

GOD IS IN THE TRIAL WITH US!

The next morning I prayed about this and asked, "Is that how You really are toward us, when we go through trials? Are You a God who sends trials and is hovering over us from a distance, grading us on how we do as we go through them?"

God answered me and *said*, "I am not a God who is distant from you. When you go through a trial, I am right there *in* the trial with you!" I thought about His response and I felt foolish in asking such a silly question in the first place. I thought, "Of course, You are in the trial with us, otherwise, we would never be able to get through it!" I remembered the verses that say, "I can do everything through HIM who gives me strength" (Philippians 4:13), and "apart from HIM we can do nothing" (John 15:5). He gently reminded me that He is *always* "for me" and that my enemy is also His enemy as well! He helped me to see that He is always in this fight with me all the way!

God reminded me of the story of Shadrach, Meshach and Abednego. These three men were thrown into a fiery furnace because they refused to bow down and worship King Nebuchadnezzar. When the king and all those around looked into the furnace, they saw "FOUR men walking around in the fire, UNBOUND AND UNHARMED, and the fourth looked like a SON OF THE GODS" (Daniel 3:25).

That is such a wonderful reminder that the Lord goes through our trials with us. He is *in it all the way!* In this story, the three men were taken out of the furnace and the king saw that "the fire had not harmed their bodies, nor was there a hair of their heads singed; their robes were not scorched, and there was NO SMELL OF FIRE ON THEM!" (Daniel 3:27).

The Lord not only went through the trial with them, but also protected them and delivered them. He gave them the victory, even to the point where they did not even smell like fire!

Count It All Joy!

Then God brought this verse to my mind:

> Consider it pure joy, my brothers, whenever you face trials of many kinds, because you know that the testing of your faith develops perseverance. Perseverance must finish its work so that you may be mature and complete, not lacking anything.
> James 1:2-4

To be honest, I never really liked that verse. I didn't like to hear how trials were good for me. I had heard many sermons about this verse and I always left feeling as if God was out to try me and test me with bad things in my life.

God began to speak to me about this verse and showed me that I just didn't have the right perspective. When James wrote this verse, He not only knew God's love for him but He also knew God's power for him. That's the reason that he could write to "count it all joy," instead of "grin and bear it."

James was the brother of Jesus, and I am sure that he watched Him through the years and saw how He handled difficult times. These difficult times put Him to the test, but it was not God testing Him. It was the enemy who was behind the temptations and the persecutions. These temptations and persecutions did test His strength and faith but they were brought about by the enemy, not God. James saw Him do miraculous things and watched His peaceful countenance as He faced trials in His life. He watched how Jesus came out of each and every trial with victory!!

That morning, God gave me a *picture* to clarify this. It was a picture of a fight. In the fighter's ring were two men. One was

obviously larger and a lot stronger than the other one. God *asked* me this question, "What does the fighter who *knows* that he is going to win often say to the other fighter?" As I contemplated this, the answer that I *heard* inside was, "C'mon, give me your best shot!" THAT'S the perspective from which James wrote that scripture, "count it all joy," because he *knew* that no matter what trial came his way, he was the victor! He knew this not just in his head but in his heart, that no matter what the enemy threw at him, he was going to win! He *knew* the love of God and his position in Christ!

In regard to persecution, he also knew that the end result would be people coming to know Jesus as their Lord and Savior. Not only was he going to win the battle, but there would be a *harvest of fruit* as a result. He counted that as "joy!" Just as Jesus did— who "for the JOY set before Him endured the cross" (Hebrews 12:3). Jesus focused on what was *after* the cross, in the many people who would be forgiven and go to Heaven because of what He went through. James also counted the wonderful things that resulted from any persecution he went through as "joy"!

It's a Fixed Fight!

James was not afraid of trials because he *knew* that he was not just a conqueror; he was "more than a conqueror"! (Romans 8:37). He *knew* that he was no longer under "the dominion of darkness" (Colossians 1:13,14), and that "the One who was in him was greater than the one who was in the world" (1 John 4:4). He *knew* that Satan was under his feet because he had been "raised up in the heavenly realms in Christ Jesus" (Ephesians 2:6,7), and that this was his position of "authority to overcome all the power of the enemy" and that "nothing would harm him" (Luke 10:19). James *knew* that God was "for" him not "against" him (Romans 8:31) and that God who sent His only Son for him would "graciously give him all things" (Romans 8:32). James *knew* that he "no longer lived, but Christ lived in him" (Galatians 2:20). He *knew* that he had a big God who lived in him through the power of His Holy Spirit and that God was bigger than any problem that he would ever face!

God showed me that I could actually look at a trial as a fixed fight. A fixed fight is one where the winner is chosen BEFORE the fight begins. Each one of us is the chosen winner. We need to see ourselves that way no matter what kind of trial we are facing. Isn't that great news? We are chosen to be victorious before the trial even begins!

God has been trying to impress upon me the importance of looking at trials like that. Instead of getting all upset and fretful when I face a trial, I am to maintain peace by knowing in my heart that nothing is going to happen during the day that God in me cannot handle!

Sometimes when people go through trials they will use the common expression, "If only I could see the light at the end of the tunnel!" However, as Christians, even if we do not *see* the light at the end of the tunnel, we *know* by faith that it is there! We know that God's Word is true and it says that He "delivers us from ALL of our troubles" (Psalm 34). It says that *four* times in just one Psalm!

> *This poor man called, and the Lord heard him; he SAVED him out of ALL HIS TROUBLES.*
>
> vs. 6

> *The angel of the Lord encamps around those who fear Him, and HE DELIVERS HIM.*
>
> vs. 7

> *The righteous cry out, and the Lord hears them; He DELIVERS them from ALL THEIR TROUBLES.*
>
> vs. 17

> *The righteous man may have many troubles, but the Lord DELIVERS him FROM THEM ALL.*
>
> vs. 19

I guess God wanted to make sure that we did not miss that. There *is* a light at the end of the tunnel! It is there and we can know it as Christians even when we don't have the slightest glimpse of it yet!

It's Just a Sparring Match!

God showed me that not only is a trial like a fixed fight, but it is also like a sparring match. What is a sparring match? It is a practice fight. It is a time when an athlete gets a chance to exercise his muscles and practice using his skills. Its purpose is to help the athlete improve and get better at what he does. A trial is like a sparring match for us as Christians because it is a time for us to exercise our spiritual muscles and to practice using our faith. Our faith is put to work. Then what happens?

> *...because you know that the testing of your faith develops PERSEVERANCE. Perseverance must finish its work so that you may be MATURE and COMPLETE, NOT LACKING ANYTHING!*

That is so exciting to think about. We grow in "perseverance," becoming "mature and complete, not lacking anything." God's power is so great that He can actually take what Satan meant to use against us, and turn it right around and bring good out of it. God throws it right back in the enemy's face by using these times to make us even stronger!

I used to think that my faith would grow as I went through trials. But the Bible says:

> *Faith comes from HEARING the message, and the message is heard through the WORD OF CHRIST.*
>
> Romans 10:17

In other words, faith comes by the Word of God. That verse doesn't say anything about trials. If faith came from trials, then people who had a lot of trials in their lives would be very strong in their faith. I have met many people who have had hard lives, and unfortunately, many of them are cold, bitter, defeated, and without hope. On the other hand, I have seen people go through hard times but use their faith as they go through them and come out strong! They have built up their faith by seeking God's Word during these times and that is what made all of the difference. They have used their faith to stand on God and His Word to get them through.

It's the Word of God that causes our faith to "come" and rise up within us. If we need our faith to spring into action, it will as we read the Word of God. Trials, on the other hand, just put our faith to the test. The enemy comes at us and our faith is tested. We need to get out our "sword," which is the Word of God, and this will help our faith as it is being put to the test by this trial.

Faith is not increased during trials, unless during those trials, we are getting into the Word of God more. What does increase during trials is perseverance. That word is used a lot in the Bible. The word means that we will not grow weary, we will be patient, we will not give up, we will persist in using our faith no matter how long it takes. We become *stubborn* Christians in a good way (smile) in that we will stubbornly never surrender to the enemy! We know that the victory is promised to us so we will never give up.

Jesus Is Our Coach to Help Us Persevere

Can Christians fail during trials? Sure they can! The victory is promised to us but Christians can grow "weary and lose heart" (Hebrews 12:3). They can give up and stop persevering. We all have a free will to use, even in the midst of a trial. However, as I have gone through trials, I have found the Lord to be my coach. A good coach will encourage and spur on the players on his team. He is my coach and the best coach! I know that He is with me and will keep me strong to get the victory every single time!

As we go through one trial, we are better prepared for the next thing that the enemy throws at us. As we come out with the victory in one trial, we know that we will come out with victory in the next trial.

The Bible says that Jesus was led into the wilderness by the Holy Spirit where He was tempted by Satan. Jesus overcame him all three times when Satan tried to tempt Him. This helped to prepare Jesus for the hardest thing that He had to go through. He had to go to the cross, and He was tempted again by the enemy to not go. The Bible says that He even sweat drops of blood as He dealt with this in the Garden! Because He persevered in the desert, He was better able to persevere in the Garden! As I persevere in one trial, I will be better able to persevere in the next thing I face.

God is so great! He takes what the enemy tries to do to us and makes us "mature and complete, lacking nothing." I have started confessing that truth, even in the middle of a trial, because it helps me to focus on the finish line. It keeps me persevering, knowing that the victory is mine and I am going to be even stronger as I cross that finish line.

God Was Not behind the Trials

Just because God brings good out of trials, it does not mean that these trials were His will or that He *allowed* them. God loves us and does not want us to be harmed or hurt in any way!

Suppose a young boy was sadly killed in an automobile accident. His funeral was so moving that five of his relatives received Jesus as their Lord and Savior. His parents, who were distant in their relationship with God, grew stronger and became people who lived for the Lord in a mighty way. Many people would look at all that and think, "It must have been God's will for that little boy to die because of all the GOOD that came out of it!"

NO, it wasn't the will of God for a little boy to be killed. God loved that little boy and He grieved the day he was killed. God grieved for the little boy as well as for his parents and all those who loved him. Yes, God lovingly took the little boy to Heaven, where he is now fine, but it was not His will for the little boy to die at such a young age. Yet, God is so great that He can take what the enemy meant for evil and turn it around for good! In this case, God turned it around to work in the little boy's family. If we see calamities come in people's lives, we need to be praying and believing that God will turn it around and use it for good somehow.

I have heard many people blame God for the bad things that have happened in their lives. They have been angry with Him about loved ones who have died, about sickness in their lives, about misfortunes and hard times. Then there are some people who say that they are not *mad* at God, but there is resentment toward Him because they believe that He *allowed* these bad things to happen to them. Inwardly, they distrust Him and wonder what other bad things He will *allow* in their lives. It hurts their relationship with Him, their faith, their trust in Him, as well as their love for Him.

I've heard some people, who feel that God is behind the bad things that have happened, say that they are going to ask Jesus about them when they get to Heaven. They are going to ask Him why He *allowed* these things to happen, or why He did not *stop* them. They wonder, "Why did my mother die when I was 8 years old?" or "Why did I injure my leg, which kept me from pursuing my dream of skiing?" or "Why did I lose all that money when that thief broke into my house?" or "Why did my husband leave me for another woman?"

Truly, I don't believe that these people will even be able to get the words out of their mouths when they see Jesus. They are going to stand in front of Jesus, look into the eyes of the One who loves them purely and perfectly, and *instantly* know that He had *nothing* to do with causing or purposely allowing those things to happen to them! They will *realize* that He loved them with a love that "surpassed knowledge" all the days of their lives! They will look into His eyes and get a revelation of His heart like they never knew when they were alive—but now know.

HIS WORD SHOWS US HIS WILL NOT OUR CIRCUMSTANCES

If we want to find out God's will about something that is happening in our lives, we need to look at God's Word. We need to look at the Bible to see what He says about it. We are not to look at the circumstances in our lives or the circumstances in other people's lives to find out what His will is. In this case, we can see that the Bible says, "With long life will I satisfy you and show you My salvation" (Psalm 91:16). There is God's heart and will for that little boy as well as for us! It is His will that we have a "long" and "satisfying" life! When people die early, it shows us that somehow the enemy got in there to "kill, steal and destroy."

Many people would ask, "What about Paul? He died early." First of all, he died because of persecution—he gave his life for Christ and not because of some accident. There are many Christians who died for the gospel. He also spoke about impending death and made statements that he was ready to go! He wrote, "I have fought the good fight, I have FINISHED THE RACE, I have kept the faith" (2 Timothy 4:7). Paul was "satisfied" and he "desired to depart and be with Christ" (Philippians 1:23).

God taught me to always look at His Word to find out what His will is, and not the circumstances in my life or other people's lives. One day, He clarified this to me. I had been reading Psalm 91. I had gotten to the verse that says:

For He will command His angels concerning you to guard you in all your ways; they will lift you up in their hands, so that you will not strike your foot against a stone.

vs. 11,12

At this time in my life, my daughter was a toddler, just learning how to walk. I thought, "Lord, how can this verse be true? My daughter falls down all the time!" I realized that my daughter was just learning how to walk, but then I thought about the times I had fallen down! I wondered out loud to the Lord how this verse could be true.

The Lord was so patient with me and gently *said*:

"Do not try to make My Word fit your life, but BY FAITH MAKE YOUR LIFE FIT MY WORD!"

What He told me changed my life. I knew that I was not to look at my life to find out God's will and to question His Word. His Word is the Truth and I can always rely on it to tell me what His will is for my life. Instead, I needed to use my faith to make my *life* come up to meet His *Word*! I needed to stand by faith that His Word was true for my life and, in doing so, I would see my life change to conform to it!

PERFECT LOVE CASTS OUT FEAR

Many people get into such fear when they are faced with trials. That is one of Satan's number one weapons. He wants us to fear, because that will hinder our faith and give him an advantage. The Bible says:

For God hath not given us the spirit of fear; but of power, and of love, and of a sound mind.

2 Timothy 1:7; KJV

Fear is the opposite of faith. In order for us to stand by faith during a trial, we need to get rid of the fear. Many times in the Bible, God told His people to not fear nor be afraid. This was not just a suggestion, but rather a commandment. In order for His people to receive from Him and be able to do all that they had to do, they needed to stand by faith!

How do we get rid of fear? Since it is a spirit, one thing that we can do is "bind" it up and then "loose" the spirit of peace to flow in our lives (Matthew 16:19). However, to prevent fear from taking root in our lives, we need to know the love of God! Yes, the more we are "rooted and established" in the love of God, the less likely we will be afraid!

> There is NO FEAR in love; but perfect love CASTETH OUT FEAR! He that feareth is not made perfect in love.
>
> 1 John 18; KJV

God's love for us is perfect! As we understand that God is always "for us" and loves us with a love that "surpasses knowledge," we will not fear! We will know that whatever comes our way, our Father will take care of us and see us through. He is *bigger* than any problem, *greater* than any mountain, and He will always be there to help us because *He loves us!*

GOD IS STILL MOVED WITH COMPASSION

So, what is God's heart for you and me as we go through trials? What is He thinking and what is He feeling? The Bible says that God is the "Father of COMPASSION and the God of ALL COMFORT, who comforts us in all our troubles" (2 Corinthians 1:3,4). Compassion means that He feels our pain with us. He does not just watch, emotionless, as we go through difficult times, but instead He hurts with us, aches with us, and grieves with us because He loves us so much. God goes through all of those times with us!

Another verse says that He is "touched by the feeling of our infirmities" (Hebrews 4:15). God is "touched" or "moved" by what we are feeling and how we hurt. The Bible talks about Jesus and what He felt when He saw the crowds of people who were hurting. It says:

When Jesus landed and saw a large crowd, He had COM-PASSION on them and HEALED their sick.

Matthew 14:14

Jesus was "moved with compassion" when He saw the sick and those who were in need. He was *so* moved with compassion that He did something about it! He healed their sick! That is not just for back then, it is the same for us today. He is the "same yesterday, today and forever" (Hebrews 13:8), and so therefore He is *still* moved with compassion when He sees us hurting in any way. That is the heart of God for you and me when we go through trials.

MY DAD'S
HOMECOMING

*M*y Dad went home to be with the Lord about two years ago. It was a difficult ordeal for him as well as for the whole family. The Lord showed me so much of His heart throughout this time.

I remember driving home in a snowstorm one evening after I had visited with Dad. It was a beautiful wintry night—snow covered everything and the sky was full of large powdery-white flakes. As I drove along, I prayed for Dad, who was battling cancer and who had gone through times of great pain. The Lord led me to think of my grandfather, my dad's father, who passed away a number of years ago. (He was 101 years old when he died!) I thought, if he were here right now and could see Dad and what he has been going through, it would *break his heart!* To watch his son, his youngest of four children, go through this horrendous experience would be heart-wrenching! I thought about what it would be like if he were sitting by Dad's bedside, and I wept.

As I continued to think about this, God intervened and softly *said*, "I am your Dad's Heavenly Father and I am constantly at his bedside. Watching him go through this is breaking *My* heart!" As I thought about what God said, I realized how much deeper His love is for my Dad than even his own father's love. How God is "touched by our infirmities," even more than anyone else. The tears flowed as I drove along on that winter night, as I thought about God's heart for my Dad and all that He was feeling.

Dad went through several more weeks, battling the cancer, after that night. I was with him when he died. He peacefully took his last breath and he was gone, home to be with the Lord. I felt more of a sense of relief than of sadness when he died, because I was thankful that the ordeal was over and he wasn't in any more pain. He was at peace and with His Lord.

SO WHY DID HE DIE?

I know in my heart that it was *not* God's will to take Dad home so early. The Bible talks about "long" and "satisfying" lives (Psalm 91). God desires to give us all a long and satisfying life. He is "no respecter of persons." My Dad was only 72 years old. In my heart, I feel as if he also had a ministry that never got fulfilled in his life because it had been cut off like this.

I don't have all the answers as to why he died and was not healed, but I do know that it was God's heart to heal him. Many people would look at his death and say, "See, it *must* have been God's will for him to die since he died!" I have learned that not everything that happens in my life or other peoples' lives is necessarily the will of God. God gets blamed for so many things that happen when it is actually due to the enemy or possibly because of our inability to receive what He desires us to have. We are to find out God's will, not by what happens in our lives, but rather by looking at His Word! The circumstances of our lives should not dictate to us what His will is, but rather His Word! In His Word we discover His very heart!

Even though I do not have all of the answers as to why my Dad died, I do have enough to give me some understanding. My

Dad was a new Christian who accepted Jesus as his Lord and Savior months before he died. Even though he believed in God most of his life and went to church regularly, he had a difficult time receiving Jesus as His Lord and Savior. He always felt as if he wasn't worthy to be a Christian and just not good enough. Since he had such a hard time receiving his salvation, I believe that receiving healing was even more difficult for him.

As a family, we would often try to explain that *nobody* is worthy or good enough and that salvation is a "free gift" (Ephesians 2:14) from God that we cannot "earn" but are to receive by "faith." It is "by grace through faith" that we are saved. As Dad grew up, so much of what he had was due to his accomplishments and hard work. He always had a hard time receiving anything for free. He felt as if he had to earn it. Dad always worked hard for what he received in life and if anyone tried to give him something, he would insist on paying for it. He had a hard time receiving anything! As a family we were thrilled when he finally understood God's free gift and personally received Jesus as his Lord and Savior. It is so wonderful to know that he is with the Lord and that I will indeed see him again and spend eternity with him.

Not only did Dad have difficulty receiving, but he often said things that were negative concerning his health and his life. He often said that he would probably get cancer someday since others in his family had it and it ran in his family. We can read in God's Word how what we say with our mouths does indeed affect our lives, either positively or negatively. The "power of life and death is IN THE TONGUE" (Proverbs 18:21).

My Dad had also said several times before he died that he "just wanted to go home and be with the Lord." He was tired of fighting and had given up. Even the doctors were amazed to see that his health went quickly downhill once he started to say that.

During the last few weeks of his life, he suffered a lot with pain as well as the emotional distress of being unable to move and therefore so completely dependent on others. I often thought this was harder on him than the pain. He had always said that he never feared dying but he feared being dependent on others since he was such a strong, independent person. I felt sad to see that "what he feared came upon him" (Job 3:25) in the end, and I could see how that fear had also been detrimental to him.

All of these things are possibilities in explaining why my Dad died. Someday when I get to Heaven, I'll have all the answers to this and everything else. God showed me that the most important thing is knowing His heart for Dad. The most important thing is knowing that God *did* want Dad healed and healthy and enjoying a "long and satisfying" life. If I had not come to terms with knowing His heart, it would have affected me later, watering down my faith if I was called to pray for someone else who was sick, or even myself. I needed to know that God's heart was for healing and for a "long" and "satisfying" life.

How Much More God Grieved

One of the hardest things I have ever gone through in my life was to watch Dad suffer, especially the last days of his life. He was in the hospital for several days. My family took shifts staying with him around the clock. There were always two people with him. We had one cot set up in the room and we would take turns resting. The longest I stayed before returning home was two days. By the end of that time, everything in me was screaming to get away from the situation and the pain I was feeling for my dad. I couldn't stand watching him suffer. However, a part of me didn't want to leave him, because I wanted to be there for him.

At his memorial service, I did not weep much. It seemed like the only times I cried were the times when others came over to me and started to cry. My tears were more of an expression of compassion for them than any grief for my Dad. Heaven is so real to me. I know that it is not some fairy-tale place but a very beautiful place where Dad now lives. I knew that he was in a much better place than I was. I even knew that if he were given the choice to either stay in Heaven or return to his life on earth, he would certainly choose to stay in Heaven. The Bible says:

No eye has seen, no ear has heard, no mind has conceived what God has prepared for those who love Him.
1 Corinthians 2:9

I had such a peace in my heart because I not only knew where he was, but I knew that I would see him again. I knew that I would again be able to talk with him, hug him, and enjoy being with him—for eternity!

Several weeks after Dad died, God gave me a deeper revelation of His heart concerning him. It happened as I was preparing for a prayer meeting at church. I had arrived at the church early and decided to pray silently before the prayer meeting began. As I bowed my head to pray, God brought my Dad to mind and reminded me of those days at the hospital and the grief I had felt for him. Then He spoke these words so clearly to me, "You think you grieved, *how much more I grieved!*" As I sat there, a flood of grief filled my heart like never before and I began to cry uncontrollably. I wept and wept and wept, as God revealed His grief for my Dad.

I realized that whatever amount of grief I had felt for Dad was NOTHING in comparison to God's grief. I could leave and get some relief from my grief after two days, but God *never* left my Dad. He was there twenty-four hours a day, night and day, feeling his pain, His heart breaking with every moan and cry my Dad would make. How He grieved for my Dad. That night God gave me a taste of the pain and the grief that He felt for him.

WE ARE THE LIFTER OF GOD'S HEAD

One week later, as I was making supper, I started thinking about what God had told me that night about His grief. Then God brought to mind the day before my Dad died. My husband had called from work and said that he felt like it was imperative that we get the family together to worship God in Dad's room. (Dad had come home from the hospital the day before because it was his wish to be home.) What was odd is that my husband cannot sing at all and is unable to stay on key. He will often not sing at church but will just stand and listen as songs are sung.

My husband left work early and we all sat around Dad's bed and sang and worshipped God. Even though Dad could not move or speak at this time, I knew that he could understand what was going on around him. I knew that he was pleased with our singing. To be honest, my initial thought when my husband called was that we were going to do spiritual warfare and that God who "inhabits the praises" (Psalm 22:3 KJV) of His people was going to powerfully work in this situation and Dad would be healed. But I was wrong—Dad died in the early hours of the morning the next day. Even so, I thought, what a beautiful way to usher him into heaven by singing sweet praises to God.

As I stood there making supper, God *asked* me this question, "Do you know the reason why I asked you to worship and sing songs to Me that day?" I thought about it and answered Him by saying, "No, what was the reason?" He *responded*, "Because I grieved so much for your Dad. *My* heart was breaking for him and all that he was suffering...the worship was to lift *Me* up."

I stood there and cried, tears dripping into the spaghetti sauce that I was stirring on the stove. I prayed, "God, please forgive me. I never thought about all that *You* were feeling for my Dad. I was more wrapped up with my own feelings for him. I was more wrapped up with my Dad's feelings, my Mom's feelings, and my family's feelings. I'm sorry."

I thought about what God had said and then I prayed, "God, You say in Your Word that You are the 'lifter of *our* head,' (Psalm 3:3) but who is the lifter of *Your* head? God, who makes You feel better when You are hurting? God, I want to be the lifter of *Your* head. Help me to be more conscious of what You are feeling and what is on Your heart. I want to lift You up with my praises, I want to make You feel better with my love…I want to bless You!"

Since that night, I have thought about the many times when God has used my own children to lift me up. As parents, we are always giving to our children, providing for them and lifting them up when they have a bad day. I started to make note of the times when I was feeling low, and either my son or daughter would come up and give me a hug, or one of them would say, "I love you, Mom," or my son would say as he typically does, "Mom, you're the best!" It is so true that our own children can lift us up when we are feeling low, and that is also true when it comes to our Heavenly Father's children—us! We can lift Him up when He is hurting.

As I drove to church that night for the weekly prayer meeting, I thought about the things God was revealing to me about His heart. I wept again just thinking how God cared enough about me and my relationship with Him to reveal more of Himself to me as He did—that He would show me what was in His heart. I thought, "Who am I, Lord, that You, the Almighty God, would make Your heart open and vulnerable to me?" I was in awe that He would care enough about me or any of us to show us these personal things about Himself. I prayed, "God, help me to be more sensitive to You, to Your feelings and to what is on Your heart. I'm so programmed to be concerned about my own needs, thinking that you as God have none."

I realized that I am nobody *special* that He would want only me to know about His heart. God wants us *all* to know His heart. He wants us *all* to know what He is feeling inside—He wants us *all* to know Him intimately. When we are having a bad day, He wants to lift us up…and when He is hurting, He longs for us to know what is on His heart and to lift Him up!

SHARING IN
HIS SUFFERINGS

*W*hen we enter into an agreement with someone, we want to know all of the terms of that agreement. We want to read the fine print and understand not just all that we will gain from it, but also all that is expected of us. How much will it cost us? What are we required to do?

There are so many wonderful benefits of being a Christian—so many beautiful promises that our loving Father gives to us. However, the Bible also talks about suffering and how there is a kind of suffering that we as Christians are supposed to "share in." What are those sufferings? As a Christian, I wanted to know exactly what those sufferings were!

> *I want to know Christ and the power of His resurrection*
> *and the fellowship of SHARING IN HIS SUFFERINGS,*
> *becoming like Him in His death, and so, somehow, to*
> *attain to the resurrection from the dead.*
> Philippians 3:10,11

What does this mean to "share in His sufferings?" Did His sufferings include things like cancer, heart attacks, poverty, birth defects, injuries, etc.? God led me to look at His Word to find out how Christ did suffer and what that verse really meant.

As I searched through the gospels, I never read how Jesus was ever sick. In fact, I never even read that He had a slight cold! I never read anything about injuries that He sustained apart from being whipped and going to the cross for our sins. So, therefore, sickness was not one of His sufferings.

I never read anything about poverty either. I used to think that since He was born in a manger, He was poor, but look who came days after His birth! The three wise men came and they surrounded Him with gifts of "gold, incense and myrrh" (Matthew 2:11). God provided *abundantly* for Him when He was born!

I used to think that He was poor when He did His ministry, but He had a treasurer who took care of the money and even gave money away to the poor! He must have had enough for Himself and all of His disciples if He was giving money away! Then when it came time to eat, it was recorded in the Bible that He multiplied five loaves and two fish to feed not only Himself and His disciples but also over five thousand people who were following Him. He fed them even to the point where they were full! To top that off, there was even food left over! When it came time to pay taxes, He had money provided for Him that came by way of a fish. He always had enough!

So what does that verse really mean? What are "His sufferings"? As I looked through the life of Jesus, I found two.

PERSECUTION

Persecution is one of the ways in which Jesus suffered, and He informs us that since they persecuted Him, they will also persecute us as Christians. Jesus said:

Remember the words I spoke to you: "No servant is greater than his master." If they persecuted Me, they will persecute YOU also. If they obeyed My teaching, they will obey yours also. They will treat you this way because of My name, for they do not know the One who sent Me.

John 15:20,21

God calls us to actually look at this kind of suffering as a privilege:

Dear friends, do not be surprised at the painful trial you are suffering, as though something strange were happening to you. But REJOICE that you participate in the sufferings of Christ, so that you may be OVERJOYED when His glory is revealed. If you are insulted because of the name of Christ, you are BLESSED, for the Spirit of glory and of God rests on you. If you suffer, it should not be as a murderer or thief or any other kind of criminal, or even as a meddler. However, if you suffer as a Christian, do NOT BE ASHAMED, but PRAISE GOD that you bear that name.

1 Peter 4:12-16

SUFFERING IN THE FLESH

The second way that Christ suffered was in His flesh. What that simply means is that He said no to His flesh and yes to God and that His flesh suffered each time that He did.

Forasmuch then as Christ hath suffered for us IN THE FLESH, arm ourselves likewise with the same mind: for he that hath SUFFERED IN THE FLESH hath ceased from sin; that he no longer should live the rest of his time in the flesh to the LUSTS of men, but to the WILL OF GOD.

1 Peter 4:1,2 KJV

We can all relate to this, even in little things like when our flesh wants a second or *third* helping of chocolate cake! (smile) If we followed every whim of the flesh, we would all be very overweight! We can relate to this when we get angry and our flesh wants to say things that we shouldn't. When we hold our tongue and keep it from speaking, our flesh suffers. We are called to follow after the Spirit and not after the flesh. The Spirit will always tell us what is right to do, while the flesh will often lead us into sin. Jesus had a flesh as well and He also had to say no to it. When He did, His flesh suffered.

We see Jesus doing that in the desert when He was fasting and Satan was tempting Him. I'm sure that His flesh wanted to eat, but He said no to it for forty days! Jesus made a practice of saying no to His flesh and yes to God. He did not let His flesh dictate to Him what He should do, but rather took authority over His flesh and told it what to do! God's Word says:

> *Although He was a son, He LEARNED OBEDIENCE from what He SUFFERED and once MADE PERFECT, He became the source of eternal salvation for all who obey Him and was designated by God to be high priest in the order of Melchizedek.*
>
> Hebrews 5:8-10

Jesus "learned obedience" by saying no to His flesh and yes to God. He was already perfect in that He was sinless, so this word *perfect* had to do with growing up and getting stronger in being able to *always* say no to the flesh and yes to God. Many people don't realize that Jesus had a choice to either say yes or no to His flesh! We can see this perfection taking place in the desert and all the way to the Garden as He chose to say no to His flesh and yes to God. In His flesh, He did not want to die on the cross. He prayed, "My Father, if it is possible, may this cup be taken from Me" (Matthew 26:39). We are all thankful that He did not choose to follow His flesh, but follow His Father.

JESUS KNEW SOMETHING
THAT WE NEED TO KNOW

I always thought this verse was just expressing how Jesus did not want to go to the cross. I realized later that Jesus made a very important statement, which was based on how well He *knew* the Father's heart. He *knew* that if there was another way for people to be saved that did not include His suffering, then God would have led Him in *that* direction instead! Jesus *knew* that God did not want Him to suffer at all. It broke the Father's heart to see His Son suffer and be crucified on that cross! God would not want this to happen if there was any other way for people to be saved. Jesus was expressing something that He *knew* about the Father's heart—something that we all need to know as well!

In Isaiah 53:10 (KJV), it says, "Yet it pleased the Lord to bruise Him…" In the following verse it explains why it "pleased" Him to have Jesus dies on the cross—"for by His knowledge shall my Righteous Servant justify many, for he shall bear their iniquities." It "pleased" God because it made a way for us to be forgiven and have eternal life! God was not "pleased" as He watched His One and Only Son suffer and die on that cross. He was "pleased" with what would happen because of it! Why? Because God "so loved the world"—He loved us!

God will only call us to suffer if there is a purpose to it and if there is no other way! We need to ask Him as Jesus knew to ask Him, "Is there any other way for this to be accomplished, than by me having to suffer?" If there is, God will tell us and lead us in that direction because He does not want us to suffer need-lessly. God suffers when we suffer because He loves us so much!

If there is no other way for people to be saved or helped, then God *asks* us if we will do it. He does not want us to respond grudgingly or under compulsion but rather out of our love for Him. Many times I have *heard* Him ask, "Will you do it for Me?" Every time I *hear* Him ask me that, it melts my heart because I know His love and all that He has done for me. When I respond with, "Yes Lord, I will do it for You," I know that melts *His* heart!

Paul is a good example of a person who suffered persecution for the sake of spreading the gospel. He made this statement that "everything we do, dear friends, is for your strengthening." (2 Corinthians 12:19) There was a *purpose* for the things he endured and he made sure that people knew that the "all-surpassing power was from God" (2 Corinthians 4:7), who sustained him and delivered him when he went through these things. We never *hear* him feeling sorry for himself but rather Paul says such things as, "So I GLADLY spend for you everything I have and expend myself as well." (2 Corinthians 12:15) and "Now I REJOICE in what was suffered for you." (Colossians 1:24) I'm sure that these words melted the Father's heart!

PAUL'S THORN IN THE FLESH

To keep me from becoming conceited because of these surpassing great revelations, there was given me a thorn in my flesh, a MESSENGER OF SATAN, to torment me. Three times I pleaded with the Lord to take it away from me. But He said to me "My GRACE IS SUFFICIENT for you, for MY POWER is made PERFECT in weakness." Therefore I will boast all the more gladly about my WEAKNESSES, so that Christ's power may rest on me. That is why, for Christ's sake, I delight in weaknesses, in insults, in hardships, in persecutions, in difficulties. For when I am WEAK, then I am STRONG.

2 Corinthians 12:7-10

Was this "thorn in the flesh" one of the sufferings of Christ? Was this a suffering that God called Paul to share in? What does this verse say about it? First, it says that it was not sent by God but rather it was a "messenger of Satan." It was given to him to "torment" him—something that Satan loves to try to do! We are called to "resist" these things and that is what Paul was doing.

Why didn't God just take it away? Paul prayed *three times*! Finally God made this powerful statement, "My grace is sufficient for you, for My power is made perfect in weakness!" As I prayed about this, God showed me that what He was actually telling Paul was that He did not *have to take it away*! God was saying, "Just lean on Me and as you do, My power will be perfected in your life!" He was telling Paul to look at this situation as if it was just an anthill instead of a mountain! Why? It's because God's power would be perfected in and through Paul and would take care of it—God's power would be *more than enough*!

God was instilling faith in Paul to believe that "greater is He who is in you [in this case, Paul] than he who is in the world" (1 John 4:4; KJV). He was trying to get him to not focus on the problem or his weaknesses but rather on *His power* that was within him all along!

I thought about the Wizard of Oz and how Dorothy always had the power to return home. She went through so much trying to get back home in this movie and then at the end, she discovered that the power was there *all the time*!

Paul was also reminded that HE had authority over the evil one. Jesus does not cast out demons or "bind" up (Matthew 16:19) the things of Satan today. Before He left, He gave *us* authority to do that! We are not to ask Him to do this for us.

After God spoke to Paul about this, what was Paul's response? Did he just start to grin and bear it and accept it for the rest of his life? No! Instead, he rises to the occasion! His faith "comes" and then he *knows* that he has the victory over this thing! He is reminded of the fact that He is "more than a conqueror"!

We never hear about this "thorn in the flesh" again in Paul's writings. I guess that it is safe to assume that this was no longer a problem for him! Praise God! Paul came away from that experience with the same attitude as James when he wrote, "Count it all joy!" It was as if Paul was shouting, "Bring it on! C'mon, Satan, give me your best shot! Whatever you throw at me, I am going to throw right back in your face because God's *power is made perfect in me*!"

JESUS IS INTERCEDING FOR US

What is God's heart toward us as we "share in His sufferings" in regard to being persecuted for His name's sake and suffering in our flesh? We know that He is a God of compassion, and He hurts and aches whenever we suffer in any way. We know that as we go through these things, which are trials in themselves, that He is *in* them with us. He is there to strengthen us and help us get through them with victory! He is 100 percent "for us," 100 percent of the time!

The Bible says that Jesus "always lives to intercede for us" (Hebrews 7:25). When Jesus went to Heaven and sat down at the Father's right hand, His work was finished. Even so, He continues to intercede for us all the time!

Since Jesus also went through these same kinds of sufferings, He knows exactly how we are feeling. He totally understands what it is like! An important thing to remember is that He not only went through these sufferings, but He also had the victory over each and everyone of them. So, He knows just what it will take for us to get through them with victory as well.

For we do not have a high priest who is unable to SYMPA-THIZE with our weaknesses, but we have one who has been TEMPTED IN EVERY WAY, just as we are— YET WAS WITHOUT SIN.

Hebrews 4:15

A Third Way
That Jesus Suffered

*A*s I was finishing up this book, God showed me a third way in which Jesus suffered. He showed me that it was necessary for me to go back and insert this chapter.

Jesus not only suffered persecution and suffered in His flesh, but He also suffered every time He was "moved with compassion" for the crowds of people who were sick and hurting. He felt their pain and ached with them and for them. Jesus suffered in His heart when He felt what they were going through.

There are times when the Bible says that Jesus "wept." People do not cry unless they are hurting inside. Jesus wept when He came to the tomb of Lazarus, who was a good friend of His. He wept even though He knew that He was going to raise him from the dead. Jesus wept over the city of Jerusalem because they did not realize who He was—that He was the Son of God. He saw what was up ahead for them in the future and He felt their pain—and He cried.

As I thought about these things, I realized that this is the *only* way in which Jesus still suffers today! He is in Heaven, sitting at the right hand of God the Father. He is no longer being persecuted for who He is, and He is no longer suffering in His flesh. However, He still suffers when we suffer. When we are suffering in any way, whether from persecution or in the flesh, whether from being sick or suffering lack…He suffers as well.

When Jesus called to Saul on the road to Damascus, He said, "Saul, Saul, why do you persecute ME?" Why did He say "Me"? He wasn't being persecuted—He wasn't even there! He said that because what affected the body of Christ also affected Him. As the Christians were being persecuted by Saul, He felt their pain—He ached with them and for them. He felt their pain just as if He too were being persecuted!

The Bible says that when one part of the body of Christ suffers, the whole body suffers: "If one part suffers, every part suffers with it; if one part is honored, every part rejoices with it" (1 Corinthians 12:26). Jesus is the head of the body of Christ, and whenever we suffer in any way, He too suffers.

The reason that the Bible calls us to "rejoice with those who rejoice; mourn with those who mourn" (Romans 12:15) is because that is what Jesus is doing! We are called to have that same compassion flow through us that flowed through Jesus as He walked on this earth and that *still* flows through Jesus today! Just as Jesus was "moved with compassion" back then, He is still "moved with compassion" today. He calls us to share in this suffering as well.

Jesus is at the right hand of the Father, interceding for us with a heart full of compassion. His prayers are not distant and cold! No! His prayers are prayers that come straight from His heart. They are full of the warmth, compassion, and love that are in His heart for you and me. He intercedes for us with fervency, as if He were praying for Himself! He is praying as if *He* were the One going through the trial, as if *He* were the One who was sick, as if *He* were the One who was being persecuted…as if *He* were the One who was suffering in pain! Why? Because He is "touched with the feeling of our infirmities" (Hebrews 4:15). He loves us so much, that He feels what we are going through as if *He* were going through it as well!

One Sunday morning I was sitting in church, listening to a pastor teach about the sufferings of Christ. However, as he preached, he included all kinds of sickness, injuries, and poverty in his sermon. He encouraged those in the congregation to *embrace* those things in their lives and believe that they were *allowed* by God for a reason.

The church was full that day. As I sat there, I thought about the number of people listening who had cancer or were suffering from terrible illnesses. I thought about those facing surgery in the coming week. I thought about those struggling financially, who did not have enough to get by. I thought about those who had recently lost loved ones in tragic accidents. I thought about those who had loved ones in the hospital or who were caring for them in their homes.

As I thought about these people, I was moved to tears. I felt so sad for them because I knew that these sufferings were not from the Lord. I tried to choke back the tears, feeling embarrassed about the thought of crying. I kept telling myself, "I am not going to cry!" Then I *heard* the Lord say to me, "Yes, you will cry." He went on to *say*, "You asked to know My heart—well *this* is My heart." With that, the tears flowed down my cheeks as I felt what He was feeling that day. I bowed my head and silently cried.

Jesus no longer suffers persecution and He no longer suffers in His flesh. The only time when He suffers is when *we* suffer. The only way in which He still suffers today is when He is "moved with compassion" for you and me.

STANDING FOR MY HEALING

After I got healed from a sprained ankle, I knew that God was a healing God who desired to make me well when I got sick. As time went by, though, I started to question this and doubt that God wanted to heal me each time I got hurt or sick. You would think that once a person had been healed of something that it would be easy for them to use their faith to receive healing again. Many times this is true, but unfortunately it was not true for me.

FALLING FOR THE ENEMY'S LIES

One reason for my doubt was that I was attending a church regularly that did not believe that God always wanted to heal us. I had gone back to attending my family church after I returned home from college. I knew there were some differences from what I believed, but I thought that it would not matter much. However, it did matter. Also, I did not read the Word consistently to build my faith up and keep it strong. My faith slipped as I heard people say different things. To be honest, my relationship with God was not all that it should have been at that time in my life as well. Overall, I was not ready for this attack from the enemy when it came.

On this particular Saturday, I decided to go for a long jog. I jogged eleven miles, which was quite a lot farther than I usually jogged. I didn't feel winded at all that day and I had so much energy that I felt like I could jog forever. I could feel some soreness in my knee as I went along, but I felt so good otherwise that I chose to ignore it. When I finally did stop, I felt a sharp, knife-like pain go through my right knee. It hurt so badly! I limped about a mile back home in excruciating pain.

For weeks my knee hurt even to just walk and sometimes the pain would keep me up at night. I prayed about it continually and *tried* to believe for my healing. It gradually improved so that I could walk on it pain-free but I could not jog anymore. Every time I tried, that knife-like pain would return. I missed jogging so much. I really enjoyed it and it was one of the best ways I had found to keep my weight down and stay in shape. Jogging had become such a part of my life that it was quite discouraging to not be able to do it anymore.

As time went on, I began to blame myself for my knee injury. I began to think that it was my fault that my knee got hurt since I was running on pavement, which I knew was unhealthy for my joints. I thought how I should have stopped jogging that day when I first felt the soreness in my knee but instead, I foolishly ignored it. Therefore, I felt as if I deserved to hurt my knee and that God did not want to heal me now. I also started to think that maybe this was God's way of keeping me from jogging anymore on pavement to make sure that I took better care of my joints. I later discovered that these were all just lies from the enemy to keep me from receiving what God did indeed want for me, which was healing! The enemy did not want me well, but *God did!*

KNOWING THE TRUTH SET
ME FREE TO RECEIVE

My sister (God bless her) gave me some tapes to listen to about healing. They were full of verses in the Bible about God's power and His will to heal. I listened to them a few times and my faith started to rise up within me. "Faith comes from hearing the message, and the message is heard through the Word of Christ." (Romans 10:17) I started to hear God's truth about my knee. The more I listened to them, the more I could feel the lies that I had believed being uprooted and dug out and replaced by God's Word! God's Word started to replace those lies and I started to see how God did want my knee healthy and well!

The enemy was behind my knee injury, for he is the one who comes to "kill, steal and destroy." I knew that it was also partly my own fault because I had not taken better care of my knee that day. However, God showed me that if I had done something wrong by jogging on pavement or jogging too far that day, He forgave me for that. It didn't matter whether I sinned in ignorance or willingly, the blood of Jesus that was shed for me washed me clean! Jesus paid the price in full for my sins, so I didn't have to *pay* any more by suffering with an injured knee!

So, I got mad…real mad at the enemy because I knew that he was ultimately behind my sore knee and MAD at myself for falling for his lies! I wasted an entire year accepting this pain as part of God's plan for my life! I had *embraced* something that the enemy had done to me instead of "resisting" it!

In a huff, I put on my jogging outfit and walked over to the track (or rather *marched* with determination!). It was a gravel track, which I knew was better for my joints. I knew that God wanted me to take better care of my body when I jogged. We all need to be wise in what we do and avoid doing those things that damage our bodies.

I prayed for my knee again and spoke out the Word of God, which I knew would be a powerful way to pray. It is our "sword" against the enemy. Jesus used the Word of God as His "sword" when He encountered the enemy in the desert. He is our example of what we do whenever *we* encounter the enemy. I prayed and asked God to help me to jog two miles, which I thought would be a great start after not jogging for an entire year.

I started jogging around the track and I was amazed that my knee was pain-free! I jogged a whole mile without even a wince of pain, and it felt *so good* to be jogging again! I just praised God as I jogged along. However, when I reached exactly one mile, that knife-like pain returned. My knee hurt so badly! I stopped jogging and just began to walk around the track.

Using the Sword

Instead of giving up and saying, "Well, I guess that didn't work," I started to pray. I asked God, "What am I missing? Is there anything else that I should do?" I *knew* it was His will to heal me. I was determined to stand by faith and receive what He wanted me to have. He reminded me of something I had heard on the tapes. He reminded me that whenever I address the enemy, I need to do it *out loud*. God hears our silent prayers as well as our spoken ones, but when we address the enemy, he only hears us as we speak it out loud. God reminded me that I have "authority over the enemy" and I have the power and right to use it! So, I was very thankful that I was all alone that day at the track! (smile) I began taking authority over the enemy. I used the Word of God against him and the name of Jesus Christ!

I reminded the enemy that "GREATER is He who is IN ME than he who is in the world"! (1 John 4:4; KJV).

I reminded him that Jesus gave me "authority" and power "to overcome ALL the power of the enemy; NOTHING will harm me"! (Luke 10:19).

I reminded him that the Word of God says that if I "resist" him, he *has* to "flee"! (James 4:7).

I confessed the Word: "By His wounds 'I' HAVE BEEN HEALED" (1 Peter 2:24), and I prayed, "Oh Lord my God, I called to You for help and you HEALED ME" (Psalm 30:2), and "For 'You' are the Lord who HEALS 'ME'"! (Exodus 15:26).

I prayed over my knee again, thanked God by faith for my healing and started to jog again. Unfortunately, I jogged just a short way and the pain returned. I stopped jogging and just walked. I tried not to get discouraged and *again* I prayed and asked God, "Is there anything else that I am missing? Is there anything else that You want me to do?"

RECEIVING BY FAITH

I waited on Him for only seconds and then in His "still small voice" (1 Kings 19:12), He *said*, "This time jog, and even if you feel the pain, believe that you HAVE been healed and just keep on jogging!" He encouraged me to use my *faith*, instead of going by sight or feelings. He reminded me of Mark 11:24 where Jesus said, "Whatever you ask for in prayer, believe that you HAVE received it and it WILL be yours"!

So, off I went again. I jogged the first several steps in pain and *then* the pain completely disappeared! I kept on jogging *pain-free*, until I finished another full mile to make the two miles that I had asked God to help me to jog! I was ecstatic! I just *floated* home that day, praising my awesome God!

I still jog today, about seventeen years later. That day when God healed my knee, I promised God that I would take better care of my body. He led me to purchase a treadmill. I wore out the first one and now have an even nicer one with a cushioned base which is healthier on my joints. I keep it in my bedroom and I usually watch Christian TV shows or listen to worship music as I jog along. I have put a lot of miles on both of the treadmills and I plan to continue to put a lot *more* on in the years to come! "Thank You, God!"

KNOWING GOD'S HEART
ABOUT HEALING

I love the verse:

Praise the Lord, oh my soul; all my inmost being, praise His
holy name. Praise the Lord, oh my soul, and forget not all
His BENEFITS—
Who forgives ALL your sins
And HEALS ALL YOUR DISEASES;
Who redeems your life from the pit
And crowns you with LOVE and COMPASSION,
Who satisfies your desires with GOOD things
So that your youth is renewed like the eagles.

Psalm 103:1-5

That is such a beautiful scripture and a powerful promise for us—you and me! For a long time I wholeheartedly believed the first part of that verse. I did not have a problem with believing that God *wanted* to "forgive" me for all my sins and that He would indeed do this. However, I had a difficult time wholeheartedly believing the second part, that He *wanted* to "heal" me from "all" my diseases and that He would indeed do that as well!

As I thought about this, I realized I was not alone in this. I prayed and asked God, "Why do people have a hard time believing that it is Your will to heal them?" He answered by *saying*, "Because they do not know my *heart* concerning healing." I realized that most people don't have a problem receiving forgiveness from God because they know His heart concerning forgiveness. However, many people do not know His heart concerning healing. God talks about healing in the *same* way that He talks about forgiveness. The reason for this is because there is no difference—His heart is always to heal, just as it is to always forgive! What a wonderful God we have!

"Faith Working Through Love"

All of God's promises are ours! Doing our part to receive them simply means using our *faith*. Faith is our connection to receiving those things.

God's Word has many promises for us, but we do not just receive them automatically. They automatically *belong* to us as Christians but we do not automatically *receive* them. We need to do our part, which involves using our faith. God's heart is that we have everything He promised us in His Word. He is never holding His promises or blessings back from us; rather He is trying to get them to us! In fact, He is hurt when we do not receive all that He has for us.

Doing our part does not mean earning these things. They already belong to us if we are Christians. When we are "in Christ," we have a blood covenant with God. The things in His Word are *ours*, and God desires for us to have them as His "dearly loved children."

STANDING BY FAITH
ON THE BLOOD OF JESUS
ALONE
WE RECEIVE BECAUSE WE ARE <u>"IN CHRIST"</u>

*For no matter how many promises God has made, they are
"YES" in Christ. And so THROUGH HIM the "Amen" is
spoken by us to the glory of God.*

2 Corinthians 1:20

Most people have one or more lamps in their homes.
However, those lamps will not light up until we plug them in.
That plug is vitally important for a lamp to work. Even though it
has the capability to light up the room, it will not work until we
plug it in! Well, faith is like that plug. As we use it, we are able to
receive the things God has promised us in His Word.

We receive our salvation through faith. It is a "gift" that we
receive through our "faith" (Ephesians 2:8,9). We first find out
about salvation by reading His Word, then we pray and receive
it by faith. The way we are to use our faith is by believing it in
our *hearts* and speaking it out of our *mouths*.

*"The Word is near you; it is in your MOUTH and in
your HEART,' that is the WORD OF FAITH we are
proclaiming: That if you confess with your MOUTH,
"Jesus is Lord," and believe in your HEART that God
raised Him from the dead, YOU WILL BE SAVED. For
it is with your HEART that you believe and are justified,
and it is with your MOUTH that you confess and are
saved.*

Romans 10:8,9

Just as we receive our salvation through faith, we also receive
everything else by faith.

What exactly is faith? The Bible says:

*Faith is being SURE of what we hope for and CERTAIN
of what we do not see.*

Hebrews 11:1

Faith is essentially believing that you have something *before*
you see that you have it! Faith is believing that you can do something *before* you actually do it! Faith is believing that something
will happen *before* it happens! The Bible says:

*Whatever you ask for in prayer, BELIEVE that you
HAVE RECEIVED it, and IT WILL BE YOURS.*

Matthew 12:24

SEEING MYSELF THROUGH
THE EYES OF FAITH

There was a time in my life when I was believing for God to
help me to eat right. Even though I was never very overweight, I
struggled with trying to eat right as God wanted me to, in not
overeating and in choosing the right foods. How I loved chocolate! I used to kid around and call myself a "chocoholic" and a

"connoisseur of the best chocolates." I later learned that this was very detrimental for me to make these negative confessions about myself, and so I no longer say those things.

God was so great and led me to do some things differently and showed me verses to stand on that pertained to self-control and treating my body the way I should, as the "temple of the Holy Spirit" (1 Corinthians 6:19). A few weeks passed and I was doing quite well. I could see some results and felt so much better about the way I was eating.

One day, as I was driving along, God gave me a *picture* in my mind to show me something. This picture was of a mountain climber. I *saw* him getting to the top of the mountain and sticking a flag into the ground as a sign of victory. I got excited as I *saw* it, but I also felt a little confused. I prayed, "God, are you telling me that this is it, that I have the victory and it is over?"

He answered by *saying*, "You should have had that picture in your mind on the very first day that you started to believe for this." God was saying that I needed to *see* myself as victorious on the first day as well as on every day after that! He wanted me to *see* myself as victorious—to *see* myself as "more than a conqueror"! He wanted me to *see* myself through His Word for who I *really* was and what I could *really* do! He wanted me to *see* myself through the eyes of faith! The Bible says:

> *This is the VICTORY that has OVERCOME THE*
> *WORLD, even our FAITH!*
>
> 1 John 5:4

I learned that as I put my faith to work like that, I did see results and I got the victory! Our faith is so important. It is not just a *little* thing. The Bible says:

> *And without faith it is IMPOSSIBLE to please God.*
>
> Hebrews 11:6

God also says:

> *But My righteous one will LIVE BY FAITH.*
>
> Hebrews 10:38

> *EVERYTHING is POSSIBLE for him who BELIEVES!*
> *[has faith]*
>
> Mark 9:23

Faith is something that should characterize our lives as Christians. As we use our faith, God is so pleased with us—and I really do want to please God! It opens the door for us to do all that He called us to do and be all that He called us to be!

PUTTING OUR FAITH IN GOD AND IN HIS WORD

What do we put our faith in? God wants us to place our faith in *Him* and in *His Word*. Those are the two places where He wants us to put our faith—not in our abilities, not in luck, not in other people, but in Him and what He says in His Word.

The Bible is full of verses about people receiving things from Jesus, including many who were healed of various diseases because of their faith.

Jesus said, "I have not found anyone in Israel with such great FAITH" [...and the centurion's servant was HEALED] (Matthew 8:10).

"Jesus SAW THEIR FAITH" [...and the paralytic was HEALED] (Matthew 9:2).

"She said to herself, 'If I only touch His cloak, I WILL BE HEALED.' Jesus turned and saw her. 'Take heart, daughter,' He said, 'Your FAITH HAS HEALED YOU.' And the woman was HEALED from that moment" (Matthew 9:21,22).

"According to your FAITH will IT BE DONE TO YOU." [...and two blind men were HEALED] (Matthew 9:29).

Chapter eleven in the book of Hebrews gives us a long list of people who were commended for their faith. God did so much in their lives because of FAITH! It is faith that opens the door for God to work in our lives. Faith is our connection with Him. Faith is what makes it possible for God to do all that He wants to do in our lives and to give us all that He promised us in His Word!

THE IMPORTANCE OF KNOWING GOD'S HEART IN REGARD TO RECEIVING BY FAITH

It's so important to read God's Word to find out what His will is for our lives, so that we know what is in His heart for us. There's a passage in the Bible about a man who did not know if it was the will of God for him to be healed or not. He had heard about others being healed by Jesus and so he believed that Jesus had the *power* to heal him, but he did not know if it was His *will* to heal him personally.

> *When He came down from the mountainside, large crowds followed Him. A man with leprosy came and knelt before Him and said, "Lord, IF YOU ARE WILLING, You can make me clean."*
>
> *Jesus reached out His hand and touched the man. "I AM WILLING," He said, "Be clean!" Immediately he was cured of his leprosy.*
>
> Matthew 8:1-3

God showed me that it was important for this man to hear that it was *His will* to heal him *before* God was able to heal him. Would this man have received his healing if he chose to not believe what Jesus had said to him? Would he have been healed if he didn't believe that it was God's will to heal him?

As Christians, we need to put our faith in God's Word, not just as it pertains to His *power* to do things in our lives, but also as it pertains to His *heart* to do those things. We need to put our faith in His power but also in His willingness and His love for us! When it comes to healing we all need to hear Him *say*, "I am not only able to heal you, but I am willing to heal you and make you well!"

FAITH WORKS BY LOVE

Faith is very important to us as Christians. Jesus made a statement to the disciples saying that faith in Him was the "work" they (and WE) were called to do:

> *Then they asked Him, "What must we do to do the works God requires?"*
>
> *Jesus answered, "The WORK of God is this: TO BELIEVE [or have faith] in the One He has sent."*
>
> John 6:28,29

Placing our faith in Jesus and His Word is the "work" we are called to do. However, in order for us to truly put our faith in someone, we need to be able to trust him. We need to know that this person cares about us—we need to know that he *loves* us. It is so important for us as Christians to know God's love for us in order to place our faith in Him and in His Word.

> *For in Christ Jesus neither circumcision nor uncircumcision is of any avail, but* FAITH WORKING THROUGH LOVE.
>
> Galatians 5:6

I used to think this verse just meant that if we weren't walking in love toward others, our faith would not work well. If we were in unforgiveness or not loving others as we should, our faith would be hindered. That is definitely true but I realized that this verse means far more than that.

This verse also means that we need to know God's *love* in order to walk in *faith*. We need to know that He loves us so much and *that* is the reason He wants to work in our lives. How can we put our faith in someone who we don't believe truly loves us? We really can't. As we grow to know His love for us on a deeper and deeper level, our faith is able to work to a greater and greater degree!

God Loves Me Even When I Blow It?

*G*od is running FASTER toward ME to FORGIVE ME for my sins than I am running toward Him to be forgiven!" Those words changed my life! God showed me His heart that day as I listened to a sermon about God's forgiveness. His heart was to forgive me; He actually *wanted* to forgive me! I realized that God sent Jesus all the way to the cross to die a painful death in order to be able to forgive me for my sins! That's how much God wanted to forgive me each and every time I failed Him.

Many times in my life, I had a hard time receiving forgiveness from God. Even though I knew from God's Word that he would forgive me for my sins when I blew it, I still struggled with so much guilt. Instead of running toward God to receive His forgiveness, I found myself wanting to run *away* because I felt so guilty! I felt as if it were an imposition on Him to forgive me every time I failed. I just did not know God's heart about this.

I used to feel as if I had to beg God to forgive me for my sins. Then I realized that He was like that shepherd *going out* and *looking* for that lost sheep (ME!). That was His heart whenever I failed Him and fell into sin (Matthew 18:12-14). He wanted me *back in His arms*. He wanted to *clean me up* and be *close* to me again! That is God's heart whenever any of us blow it!

THE FATHER RAN TO THE PRODIGAL SON

I love the parable of the prodigal son (Luke 15:11-32). It demonstrates God's heart to us so beautifully. The son leaves home, wastes all of his money, spends his life in sin, and then finally comes to his senses and decides to return to his father. He realizes that he does not deserve to be treated as a son after what he has done but hopes that possibly his father will hire him as one of his servants. Instead, the father's response is so different, so full of mercy and grace...and love:

> But while he was still a long way off, his father saw him
> and was FILLED WITH COMPASSION FOR HIM;
> HE RAN TO HIS SON, THREW HIS ARMS
> AROUND HIM AND KISSED HIM.
> The son said to him, "Father, I have sinned against
> heaven and against you. I am no longer worthy to be called
> your son."
> But the father said to his servants, "Quick! Bring the
> BEST ROBE and put it on him. Put a RING on his finger
> and SANDALS on his feet. Bring the fattened calf and kill
> it. Let's have a feast and celebrate. For this son of mine was
> dead and is alive again; he was lost and is found."

God showed me that this is His response to us when we fail Him. He is not standing there with a club in His hand waiting to beat us over the head with it when we come to Him. He is not standing there ready to give us a condemning and demeaning speech as to how bad we have been. No, He is *running* toward us, *embracing* and *kissing* us and restoring us to Himself again!

As I thought about the father in the parable, I thought how that son must have smelled so bad since he had been working with pigs and probably hadn't had the money to even bathe! But that didn't matter to the father! He hugged him, stink and all! God forgives us and hugs us, stink and all, no matter what our sin has gotten us into!

The Bible says:

> *Or do you show contempt for the RICHES OF HIS KINDNESS, TOLERANCE AND PATIENCE, not realizing that God's KINDNESS leads you toward REPENTANCE.*
>
> Romans 2:4

It is knowing God's "kindness," His heart of love for us, that leads us back to Him in repentance. "There is no fear in love. But perfect love drives out fear, because fear has to do with punishment" (1 John 4:18). When we realize that His love is perfect, unconditional, unfailing, steadfast, and we are "rooted and established" in knowing His love, it will cause us to go *running* back to Him every time we sin!

THE FATHER REACHES OUT HIS HAND AND CATCHES US

I love the story about Peter when he tried to walk on the water. Jesus beckoned him to come out of the boat and walk on the water. I give him such credit because he *did* walk on the water while all of the other disciples stayed in the boat!

> *"Lord, if it's You," Peter replied, "tell me to come to You on the water."*
>
> *"Come," He said.*

> *Then Peter got down out of the boat, walked on the*
> *water and came toward Jesus. But when he saw the wind,*
> *he was afraid and beginning to sink, cried out, "Lord, save*
> *me!"*
>
> Matthew 14:30

Peter took his eyes off Jesus and started looking at the water and the waves and the wind—all of the circumstances around him. As his faith sank, he sank!

What is so beautiful is the Lord's response to Peter. He loved Peter so much. He didn't yell at him or just let him stay in the water and suffer the consequences of his failure. No, it says:

> *IMMEDIATELY Jesus REACHED OUT HIS HAND*
> *and CAUGHT HIM. "You of little faith," He said, "why*
> *did you doubt?"*
>
> Matthew 14:31

Instead of letting Peter sink, Jesus caught his hand and pulled him up to safety. That is God's response to us when we fail Him or fall into sin. When we cry out to Him for help, He reaches out to us and pulls us back up!!

Jesus paid the price for our sins in full so there is nothing left for us to pay. I used to think that I had to do something in order to receive His forgiveness. Even after I asked Him to forgive me, I would still feel like I had to do something else. However, if I still had to do something else, then it would be like saying that Jesus did not pay the price for my sins *in full*. It would be like saying that the blood of Jesus was *not enough!* His blood is enough and it is powerful enough to wash away all of my sins and all of yours as well! "The righteous requirements of the law are FULLY met in us" because of JESUS! (Romans 8:4). God says:

If we confess our sins, He is FAITHFUL and JUST and
WILL FORGIVE us our sins and PURIFY us from ALL
UNRIGHTEOUSNESS.

1 John 1:9

God is faithful and He purifies us from *all* unrighteousness—not just some, not just in part, but all unrighteousness!
Praise God! God's heart is always to forgive us! As we grow to
understand how great His love is for us, it will cause us to go
running back to Him—back to His embrace—each time we fail
Him.

Do I Have to Suffer the Consequences?

*W*hat about after we sin? Should we expect bad things to happen to us as Christians? The Bible says that a man reaps what he sows. Therefore, after we sin, should we just wait with expectant dread for the "hammer to fall" in our lives?

> *Do not be deceived: God cannot be mocked. A man REAPS WHAT HE SOWS. The one who sows to PLEASE HIS SINFUL NATURE, from that nature will REAP DESTRUCTION; the one who sows to PLEASE THE SPIRIT, from the Spirit will REAP ETERNAL LIFE.*
>
> Galatians 6:7,8

This verse concerned me. I knew that it was true and that it was a spiritual law. It said that if we kept living according to our sinful nature, we reaped destruction in our lives. Sin hindered our relationship with God and hurt our fellowship with Him. It opened the door for the enemy and made us vulnerable to him.

Previously, I mentioned how God gave me a *picture* of a fortress to explain what happens when we sin. The Bible refers to God as our "fortress" (Psalm 91). When we sin, it is like going outside of that safe fortress to a place of danger, where we are vulnerable to the enemy. I inquired of the Lord, "What happens when we repent of our sins? Does it take time to work our way back to the fortress in order to be safe again?"

He showed me that the moment I repent of that sin, I am *immediately* placed right back inside the safe walls of that fortress! Peter was *immediately* pulled back inside the safety of the boat! The prodigal son was *immediately* accepted back as a son! God does not leave us outside the fortress to suffer the consequences of our sins or our failures. His heart is to restore and protect His children from the enemy and all that the enemy tries to do to them. His heart is to deliver us from the consequences of our sins!

We Reap the Bad Consequences of Sins Before Repentance—Not After!

Before I understood God's heart about this, I thought that God wanted me to reap the bad consequences of my sin even after I had repented of them and received forgiveness. I thought God just wanted to teach me a lesson so that I would not sin again. I thought I *had* to suffer the consequences.

I realized that God's heart was not like that at all. The Bible says, "He does not treat us as our sins deserve or repay us according to our iniquities" (Psalm 103:10), and all through Psalm 136 (KJV), it says, "His mercy endures forever!"

As I looked at the parable of the prodigal son, I saw that the only reaping from his sin happened before he repented—not after! He suffered the consequences of his sin *before* he returned to his father. He reaped what he sowed in sin *before* he repented. Once he returned, the father restored him and gave him everything that he had prior to the time when he sinned! The son was not made to pay for his sins in some way or required to work off the money he had wasted. Yes, the money that he had wasted away was gone, but the father had plenty to give him when he returned! There is no implication that this son was made to suffer lack by his father because of his sin. No, Jesus was trying to show us that the penalty for his sins had been paid for *in full!* There was nothing else that he had to do or could do to be restored!

This story shows us the Father's heart toward us. He does not want us to pay a price for our sins or suffer the consequences of them. He wants us *completely restored* with *all* that He desires us to have! Once the prodigal son had asked for forgiveness and repented of that sin, he was restored and was given all that he had in his life before he ever sinned—the robe, the sandals, the ring, his sonship and even a fattened calf to celebrate! Nothing was missing, nothing was taken away, and nothing was different!

THE BLOOD CUTS OFF THE REAPING

God gave me an illustration that enabled me to see His heart a little clearer. He showed me a *picture* of a time line. The time line was of the life of someone who was in sin and it showed the reaping of bad consequences from that sin. This line continued on with reaping bad consequences *until* that person repented and asked for forgiveness. At that point on the time line, I saw a bright red line coming down perpendicular to the time line. Praise God! As it crossed the time line right at the spot where this person repented, it *cut off* the reaping of what was sown. It immediately cut off the bad consequences of that person's sin! That was the heart of God and the power of the blood of Jesus Christ!

WE NEED TO PUT OUR FAITH IN THE BLOOD!

Does everyone automatically receive freedom from the reaping of their sin after they repent? No. In fact, I used to

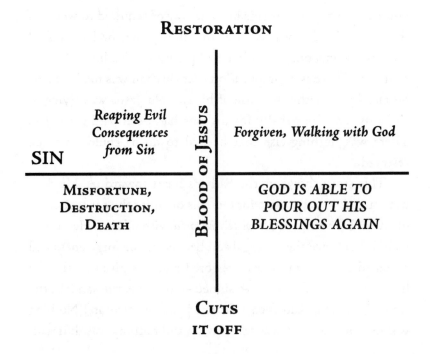

RESTORATION

	Reaping Evil Consequences from Sin	BLOOD OF JESUS	Forgiven, Walking with God
SIN			
	MISFORTUNE, DESTRUCTION, DEATH		GOD IS ABLE TO POUR OUT HIS BLESSINGS AGAIN

CUTS
IT OFF

expect that I would suffer the consequences for my sins and that God wanted to use those consequences to teach me never to do that again! Since I expected them, I was not putting my faith in the power of the blood to cut those consequences off. I was actually putting my faith in receiving bad things as a result of my sins! We need to know in our hearts that it is *not* God's will that we reap the bad things from our sins. We need to put our faith in God to deliver us from the messes that our sins get us into!

I *heard* God say this to me once and it showed me His heart when I failed. It really changed my life. He *said*:

Even if you DIG A PIT and JUMP IN IT YOURSELF, I am MORE THAN WILLING and ABLE to GET YOU OUT OF IT!

That is God's heart for me and for you. Even when we get ourselves into trouble because of sin, He is still more than willing and able to get us out of that mess!!

I waited patiently for the Lord;
He turned to me and heard my cry.
He lifted me out of the slimy pit,
Out of mud and mire;
He set my feet on a rock
And gave me a firm place to stand.
He put a new song in my mouth,
A hymn of praise to our God.
Many will see and fear
And put their trust in the Lord.

Psalm 40:1-3

God is always "for us," no matter what our sins may get us into! I love that verse:

If we are faithless,
He will REMAIN FAITHFUL,
For He cannot disown Himself!

2 Timothy 2:13

God's love is unconditional! I realized that God's love never changes for me. He doesn't love me more when I am doing things right and He doesn't love me less when I fail Him. His love and His faithfulness stay the same regardless of what I am doing. He hates the sin, but He loves the sinner! He loves me even when I blow it!

REAPING CONSEQUENCES THAT CANNOT BE CHANGED

At times we may do things that lead us into problems that cannot be changed. Suppose two people who are unmarried have an intimate relationship and a child is born. Suppose someone commits a serious crime and has to go to prison for it. Suppose a student has a fight with another student and gets expelled from school. Some consequences happen due to nature and due to the legalities in the world. The thing that is *most* important to remember is God's heart.

God's heart is for us and with us as we go through these things. He is not leaving us to suffer the consequences alone—He will get us through them. He can even turn things around and use them for our good. He doesn't leave you in that prison cell all alone, or forsake you while you are expelled from school, or leave you with no support or provision as you raise your child without a father. He will always be with us and for us to see us through!

God is always seeking to either deliver us from those evil consequences or turn them around to work good in our lives as He goes through them with us. God's heart is always to restore, deliver, sustain and help! He is always "for us." When we come to Him in repentance, asking for forgiveness, it opens the door for Him to do all that He wants to do in our lives.

The Blood Supersedes the Word!

I had a difficult pregnancy with my first child, Joshua. I was diagnosed with placenta previa early in my pregnancy. My doctor told me to just go home and stay on bedrest as much as possible. I was told that I would most likely have a miscarriage and that this baby would never be born. I returned home and prayed and believed God for a healthy baby. How I wanted to have this baby! I read and listened to the Word of God to build up my faith and to encourage me to not give up. Within three months, I was off bedrest and the placenta previa was completely gone! Praise God!

However, at almost six weeks before my due date, I went into labor. Thank God the labor stopped, but my doctor put me in the hospital for a week. They did tests and predicted that Joshua's lungs were not fully developed yet and if he were born at that time, he would weigh only four pounds. Just before I was to go back home, the labor started again. This time, it did not stop, and Joshua was born. To the doctor's amazement, his lungs were fully developed and he weighed six pounds, two ounces! Praise the Lord!

They put Joshua with the other premature babies. He certainly did stand out among all of the tiny babies there! Some of them weighed only one or two pounds. It was amazing to see how small they were and how they could survive in incubators and with the care of the medical staff. However, Joshua needed no tubes or special care—he was *huge* in comparison to them!

What touched my heart were the mothers and fathers who came in to visit their babies each day. They would stand by the incubators, lovingly looking at them. You could see in their eyes how much they longed to hold their babies and give them all the love that was in their hearts. Unfortunately, they couldn't hold them, they couldn't care for them, and they couldn't take them home. It was heart-breaking and I could feel their pain.

As I thought about it, God compared this to how He felt about us. I *saw* Him standing outside of that *incubator*, longing to be close to us and to give us everything that was in His heart, but He was unable to because of the wall of sin.

I thought about how God must have felt when Adam sinned. How everything in His heart must have wanted to *pick* Adam up and *hold* him in His arms. How He longed to be *close* to Adam again and how He longed to give Adam the comfort that he so needed at that time. However, if His holiness had come in contact with Adam's sin, no doubt Adam would have died instantly.

Then, out of His love for us, God sent His prophets to speak for Him. He reached out to us with His very Word to tell us about Himself and about the things that were on His heart. He gave us His law to tell us about holiness and what He longed for us to be like. He gave the law to us to show us what we needed to do to be protected and to receive from Him. He did so much to reveal His heart to us.

Then God showed us His plan of salvation to get us back! He told us about Jesus! He sent His very Son to make us holy so that there would no longer be an incubator wall of sin between

Him and us. God could finally be *close* to us and give us all that was in his heart!

It was through the *blood* of Jesus that He got us back! It was through His *blood* that He was able to forgive us for our sins and cleanse us from all unrighteousness! It was through the *blood* of Jesus that He was able to get rid of the wall of sin which stood between Him and us! It was through the *blood* that He was able to give us what was in His heart!

Years ago, the Lord *spoke* this word to me:

"THE BLOOD SUPERSEDES THE WORD!"

When I first *heard* Him say that, I asked, "God, did I hear you correctly?" I thought He meant that they were somehow not in agreement with each other. I thought I must be hearing Him wrong because I knew that everything needed to be in agreement—from the Word, to the blood, to the Holy Spirit. I truly questioned if I had heard Him correctly.

Then God showed me that the blood of Jesus does not go *against* the Word of God, but it goes *beyond* it! It is so powerful that it goes *farther* than the Word! The Word and the blood are in agreement but it's as if the blood picks up where the Word was unable to go! It brings about God's heart for us to an even greater degree!

The Word and the blood are on the same team. They are working together to bring us what is in God's heart. The Word takes us so far and then the blood of Jesus takes us even farther. It's as if they are playing a football game and God's heart is the football. The Word of God carries God's heart all the way down the field...to the forty-yard line...to the thirty...to the twenty-yard line! Then the Word passes the heart of God off to the blood, who then runs with it, along with the Word by its side, and crosses the goal line! TOUCHDOWN!

The blood provided the way for us to be able to receive all the things that are in God's heart! What God was saying was that the blood of Jesus was essentially the *method* that God chose to provide us with *all* that He desires for us!

Think about it. The Word could not do it alone. Where would we be without the blood of Jesus? Where would we be if Jesus had never died for us? We would still have the Word of God, but we would not have the blood covenant that we now have through Jesus. It is through that blood covenant that we are able to receive all the wonderful promises that are in His Word! The *blood* actually makes it possible for us to receive all that God wants us to have!

THE BLOOD PURCHASED THE THINGS GOD WANTS US TO HAVE

Even though there are so many wonderful promises in God's Word for us, there are also so many rules and regulations as well. God told His people to follow these in order to be prosperous, blessed, and safe. But, because of the blood of Jesus,

- we are no longer "under God's law but under GRACE" (Romans 6:15),
- we have been "JUSTIFIED by His blood" (Romans 5:9),
- and we are "RECONCILED to Him through the death of His Son" (Romans 5:10).

Because of the blood of Jesus, we can freely receive what He desires us to have. We do not have to try to earn His wonderful promises by following the law, those rules and regulations, because the blood of Jesus *purchased* them for us! The blood of Jesus paid the price for us to be able to receive these promises, and the blood of Jesus paid for them *in full!* These promises are ours through Jesus Christ. If we sin, it may hinder us from receiving them, but the promises are still ours through the blood of Jesus and that alone!

> *Therefore, brothers, since we have confidence to ENTER the Most Holy Place by the BLOOD of Jesus, by a new and living way opened for us through the curtain, that is, His body, and since we have a great priest over the house of God, let us DRAW NEAR to God with a sincere heart in full assurance of faith, having our hearts sprinkled to cleanse us from a guilty conscience and having our bodies washed with pure water.*
>
> Hebrews 10:19-22

God is no longer standing outside of that incubator, unable to *touch* us. He is no longer unable to give us the things that He desires for us. Rather, through the blood of Jesus, God can be *close* to us and *hold* us again by His Spirit. The blood made it possible for us to *draw near* to God and for God to have a close relationship with each and every one of us. The blood provided the way for God to get His heart and all that is in His heart to us!

How Does God Discipline Us?

*H*ow does God discipline us? When I do something wrong and sin against Him, how does He respond to that? I have heard so many sermons about God's discipline and they left me feeling as if He were a God who stands over us, waiting for us to make a mistake so that He can send some terrible catastrophe into our lives to teach us not to do that ever again! I knew in my heart that God was not like that—He is not harsh with His children, but rather full of tender love for us. Even so, I knew that He did indeed discipline us in some way. The following verse talks about that fact:

> *And you have forgotten that WORD OF ENCOURAGE-*
> *MENT that addresses you as SONS: "My son, do not*
> *make light of the Lord's discipline, and do not lose heart*
> *when He rebukes you, because the Lord disciplines*
> *THOSE HE LOVES, and He punishes everyone He*
> *accepts as a SON." For what son is not disciplined by his*

*father? If you are not disciplined (and everyone undergoes
discipline), then you are illegitimate children and not true
sons. Moreover, we have all had human fathers who disciplined us and we respected them for it. How much more
should we submit to the Father of our spirits and live! Our
fathers disciplined us for a little while as they thought best;
but God disciplines us for OUR GOOD, that we may
SHARE IN HIS HOLINESS. No discipline seems pleas-
ant at the time, but painful. Later on, however, it produces
a HARVEST of RIGHTEOUSNESS and PEACE for
those who have been trained by it.*

Hebrews 12:5-11

IT IS A PRIVILEGE!

First, God showed me that I need to count it a privilege
when He disciplines me! Every time He disciplines me, it shows
me once again that He really loves me and that I am a true
daughter of His. That verse says that He only disciplines those
who He loves and are really His sons and daughters! The more I
know God and His heart for me, the more I know that everything He does in my life is out of a heart full of love for me,
including discipline!

GOD'S PURPOSE: MY GROWTH

What is the purpose of discipline? Is it simply to punish us
or hurt us in some way? No, the Word of God says that the purpose of it is to produce a "harvest of righteousness and peace" in
my life and I always want more of that! His discipline will ben-
efit me immensely if I allow myself to be "trained" by it! It is
my choice. God wants to help us to grow "from glory to glory"
(2 Corinthians 3:18) to be more like His Son Jesus, who is perfect and sinless. The purpose of discipline is for us to be able to
"share in His holiness," so that we can be more like Him!

The Bible tells us how we are to deal with people who may not be living the way they should. God tells us to "gently instruct" (2 Timothy 2:25) others and to "speak the truth in love" (Ephesians 4:15). God is essentially telling us to do as He does. He desires to deal with us when we are not living the way that we should by "gently instructing" us and "speaking the truth in love." He is hoping that this will be enough to get our attention and have *us* make the corrections that need to be made in our lives.

Discipline works to change us if we "submit" ourselves to God during it and choose to be "trained" by it. We always have a free will to either submit to God and make the corrections in our lives right then and there, or we can walk away without repenting and possibly suffer the consequences of those sins. God doesn't want us to walk away in unrepentance. He doesn't want us to suffer bad things from sin in our lives. However, God will always give us that choice.

His Number One Method— The Word!

How does God discipline His children? That was what I *really* wanted to know. What could I expect from God when I got off track? Was He going to hurt me in some way?

The more I studied the Bible, the more I knew that it was Satan who brought calamity and sickness into our lives, not God. It was Satan who came to "kill, steal and destroy." This often happened as we got outside the will of God due to things like sin, fear, lack of knowledge, negative words, etc. We would get ourselves off track and outside of the safe "fortress" walls, becoming vulnerable to the enemy. Even though Satan brought these things upon us, God could still speak to us *while* we were in these messes. God could correct us *during* those bad times but it was not God who brought them upon us.

So, how does God discipline us?

For whom the Lord loveth He chasteneth, and scourgeth
every son whom He receiveth.

Hebrews 12:6 (KJV)

When I looked up the word *scourgeth* in a concordance, I saw the words "to chew and to GNAW!" The word *gnaw* gave me the image of someone who was *continually* trying to get our attention—someone who was *continually* trying to reach a deeper level within us, someone who was *continually* trying to touch our hearts! It gave me the image of Someone who was trying to show us that we were going in the wrong direction, trying to get us to turn around!

I also looked up the word *chasten*. Many of the words that were used to define it were words like "to train up a child," to "educate," to "instruct," to "learn," to "teach," to "nurture," to "correct," to "reprove," to "reform," and "tutelage." The word *punish* was also in there, but amazingly, it was surrounded by all of these other words!

As I read the following verse, I found many of the same words:

All scripture is God-breathed and is useful for TEACH-
ING, REBUKING, CORRECTING AND TRAINING
IN RIGHTEOUSNESS, so that the man of God may be
thoroughly equipped for every good work.

2 Timothy 3:16,17

As I looked at these things, I realized that the number-one method God uses to discipline us is with His Word! The Holy Spirit works hand in hand with God's Word to show us where we have sinned and missed it. This is God's *method of choice*, you might say. This is the method He desires to use, and it is His hope that it will be enough to get us on the right track.

Reading and knowing the Word of God is so important. We cannot neglect it if the Bible says that we are to be "taught, rebuked, corrected and trained" by it. Previously, we looked at what God told Joshua as He was preparing him to lead His people into the promised land:

> *Be strong and very courageous. Be careful to obey all the law My servant Moses gave you; do not turn from it to the right or to the left, that you may be successful wherever you go. Do not let this Book of the Law depart from your MOUTH; MEDITATE on it DAY AND NIGHT, so that you may be careful to do EVERYTHING written in it. Then you will be PROSPEROUS and SUCCESSFUL.*
>
> Joshua 1:7,8

In order for Joshua to be successful in doing what God called Him to do, He needed to read the Word, know the Word, put the Word in His mouth, and follow the Word of God. Then He would be able to do what God called Him to do! Then he would be "prosperous and successful."

Jesus said:

> *I am the true vine, and My Father is the gardener. He cuts off every branch in Me that bears no fruit, while every branch that does bear fruit he prunes so that it will be even more fruitful. You are already clean because of the WORD I have spoken to you.*
>
> John 15:1-3

The word *prune* actually means "clean" in the Greek. So in other words, God "cleans" you so that you can be fruitful and He does it through the Word! The Word shows you where you have missed it, and it even goes farther to "sanctify" you (John 17:17-19). The Word of God is powerful and brings change in our lives!

Then Jesus goes on to say:

If you remain in Me and My WORDS remain in you, ask
whatever you wish, and it will be given you.

John 15:7

It is the *Word* that keeps us "clean" and that "prunes" us. It is the *Word* that keeps us on track and fruitful. It is the *Word* that "sanctifies" us. It is the *Word* that keeps us in a position of obedience and therefore in a position to receive from God as long as we *hearken* to it!

REFUSING TO BE TAUGHT BY THE WORD

However, what happens to us if we refuse to be "taught, rebuked, corrected and trained" by God's Word? We all have a free will to listen and make the corrections in our lives, or to walk away in disobedience. Unfortunately, the Bible is clear that if we walk in disobedience, we will reap what we sow. It is clear that if we continue in sin, it will lead to some kind of "death" in our lives. If we refuse to listen and be obedient to God's Word, it will only hurt us.

So, does God just give up on us if we choose to disobey Him and go our own way? No, all the time, whether we are suffering from the consequences of our sins, whether we are in some pit that we got ourselves into because of our wrongdoing, whether we are a little off track or *far* off track, He is continually "gnawing" at our hearts with His love. He is continually beckoning us back to Himself! The Bible says that it is God's "kindness" that "leads" us "toward repentance" (Romans 2:5).

There are two places in the New Testament where God talks about people who did not listen and continued in not listening. These people were committing abominable sins and were unrepentant about them:

Some have SHIPWRECKED THEIR FAITH. Among them are Hymenaeus and Alexander, whom I have handed over to Satan to be taught not to blaspheme.

1 Timothy 1:19,20

When you are assembled in the name of our Lord Jesus and I am with you in spirit, and the power of our Lord Jesus is present, hand this man over to Satan, so that the SINFUL NATURE may be destroyed and his spirit saved on the day of the Lord.

1 Corinthians 5:4,5

Paul described what this "sinful nature" was:

It is actually reported that there is SEXUAL IMMORAL-ITY among you, and of A KIND THAT DOES NOT OCCUR EVEN AMONG PAGANS: A MAN HAS HIS FATHER'S WIFE.

1 Corinthians 5:1

These verses imply that these people had been approached about their blasphemy and sexual immorality, not just by God, but by other people. They had heard the Word! Even so, they had refused to repent of these things. It is not a matter of them just not knowing this was wrong; rather it was deliberate disobedience to God. They willfully made the choice to sin against God.

I could see how their sin had made them vulnerable to the enemy. In both cases, Satan was able to hurt them because they were outside of the safe walls of the "fortress." In the first case, it mentions how these men would be "taught" not to blaspheme. This verse is not saying that Satan is our teacher, because the Bible says that the Holy Spirit and the Word of God "teach" us. However, these men were taught to not sin *while* they were suffering from the results of their sin. Satan does not teach us nor does Satan *want* to teach us anything good! It is Satan's will that we keep on sinning! These men were taught not to sin by God's Word and the Holy Spirit *while* Satan had his hand on them.

What caught my attention, though, was God's heart. His heart was not to hurt them but rather to *help* them. It was God's desire that "the sinful nature be destroyed" and that they learn "not to blaspheme." It was God's hope that *while* they were in the pit as a result of their own sin, they would finally listen to Him and repent. He was still "gnawing" at them and calling them to Himself with "kindness." He had not given up on them! He was not saying, "I'm tired of your sin, get out of My sight!" No, He was longing to have a close relationship with them again. He still loved them! His love is unconditional! He loved them *just as much* as He loved them when they were living right!

These two people got outside of God's "fortress" and were vulnerable to the enemy. As I looked at these verses, I could understand how people could get confused about the will of God. It did sound as if it was God's will and heart that they be "handed over to Satan." However, the fact is that these two men were vulnerable to the enemy because of their *own sin.* That is a spiritual law that God cannot go against because He is holy and because He has given each of us a free will. Even though God "handed" them over to Satan, it was because He *had* to!

Even though God has to do this, He is reluctant. Satan is not just our enemy, but he is also God's enemy as well! What is God's heart? He is always wanting the best for us! We *see* God's heart in what He hopes will happen while these people are vulnerable to the enemy. He hopes they will repent of their sins and come back to Him! He wants to pick them up out of the pit they have gotten themselves into and be close to them again!

The Bible doesn't tell us what eventually happened to these men, although in 2 Corinthians 2, Paul seems to be talking about the man who was in an immoral relationship. He seems to imply that he did indeed repent of this sin. Did they all turn back to God? Were all of them restored in their relationship with God? Was God able to be the loving Father He desired to be in their lives once again? Hopefully they all did, which is what God's heart longed for.

Job—A Book about God's Mercy?

I have found this book in the Bible to be confusing. For a long time, it seemed like a book about a good man who did nothing wrong and yet God allowed Satan to do all kinds of terrible things to him. As I asked God to help me understand this book, He gave me revelation to see the truth about it. Not only did He help me to see His truth, but also to *see* His very heart. I thank God because now I am able to look at this book as a book about the *mercy* of God and about His *love* for this man named Job.

So, the big question is: Why did all of these terrible things happen to Job? The Bible says that he was such a good man!

"What I Feared Has Come upon Me"

The Bible is clear that sin makes us vulnerable to the enemy. It is sin that gives the enemy a "foothold" or "opportunity" to harm us. Fear is another thing that opens the door for the enemy in our lives. Fear is the opposite of faith. Faith is what opens the door for God to work in our lives, whereas fear is what opens the door for the enemy. Fear is actually putting faith in what the enemy wants to do to you—killing, stealing and destroying!

> *Job said, "What I FEARED has come upon me; what I*
> *DREADED has happened to me."*
>
> Job 3:25

There is the fear. Why it was there is unclear. It appears that Job did not have an accurate knowledge of who God was and His heart for Him. I could *see* that by the things He said about God. Many of the things that He said about God were not true. One of the things He called God was "unjust"! God is definitely a just God. There is nobody who is more just than He is! I also wondered if the reason Job had fear was because he knew that he had sin in his life. Regardless of what the reason was, it is clear that Job did have fear.

"TO HIS SIN HE ADDS REBELLION"

As I read through Job, I wondered more about sin. It wasn't as clear as seeing the fear that was there. However, the more I read about what Job said, the more I got a glimpse of Job's heart. "For out of the overflow of the heart the mouth speaks" (Matthew 12:34). The Bible essentially says that we can get a glimpse of what is in a person's heart by what he says.

By reading some of the things that Job said, I *saw* that pride was possibly a problem. Time and time again, he confessed that he was "not guilty" (Job 10:7), that he was "righteous and blameless" (Job 12:4), and that "GOD had wronged" Him (Job 19:5,6)!

Job spoke some terrible things about God simply because he did not know God and he actually made himself out to be better than God!

> *How then can I dispute with Him? How can I find words*
> *to argue with Him? Though I were innocent, I could not*

*answer Him; I could only plead with my Judge for mercy.
Even if I summoned Him and He responded, I do NOT
BELIEVE He would give me a HEARING. He would
crush me with a storm and multiply my wounds FOR NO
REASON.*

Job 9:14-17

*I will say to God: Do not condemn me, but tell me what
charges You have against me. Does it PLEASE You to
OPPRESS me, to spur the work of Your hands, while YOU
SMILE on the schemes of the wicked?*

Job 10:2,3

Job just did not know the heart of God and, therefore,
accused God of doing things that were unjust and cruel!

There were four men who talked with Job during this time.
The Bible made it clear at the end of this book that Job's three
friends did *not* speak what was pleasing to God. Elihu was the
only man who spoke what was *right* before God. Elihu was the
youngest, and he waited until these three other men were finished speaking, out of respect for them. God showed me so
much through what this man of integrity said to Job. It is clear
from what he said that Job was in sin:

*Elihu said, "Job speaks WITHOUT KNOWLEDGE; his
words LACK INSIGHT. Oh, that Job might be tested to the
utmost for answering like a WICKED MAN! To his SIN
he adds REBELLION; scornfully he claps his hands among
us and MULTIPLIES HIS WORDS AGAINST GOD.*

Job 34:35-37

*Elihu also said, "Why do you complain to Him [God] that
He answers none of man's words? For God DOES
SPEAK—now one way, now·another—though man MAY*

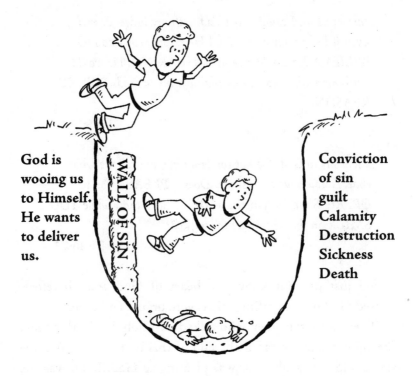

God is
wooing us
to Himself.
He wants
to deliver
us.

Conviction
of sin
guilt
Calamity
Destruction
Sickness
Death

NOT PERCEIVE it. In a dream, in a vision of the night,
when deep sleep falls on men as they slumber in their beds,
He may speak in their ears and terrify them with warnings,
to TURN A MAN FROM WRONGDOING and keep
him from PRIDE, to PRESERVE HIS SOUL FROM THE
PIT, HIS LIFE FROM PERISHING BY THE SWORD."
Job 33:13-18

There it is—"pride" and "sin"—Elihu makes it clear that
these things were in Job's life and he tried to get Job to see this.
He then encouraged Job to repent:

Should God then reward you on YOUR terms, when you
REFUSE TO REPENT? YOU must decide, not I; so tell
me what you know.
Job 34:33

There is the word *repent.* If there was no sin in Job's life, then why would Elihu say that? But, even if some might question if there was any sin in Job's life after reading all of these verses, what Job himself says at the end of this book makes the fact that he sinned clear:

> Then Job replied to the Lord: "I know that You can do all things; no plan of Yours can be thwarted. You asked, 'Who is this that obscures My counsel without knowledge?' Surely I spoke of things I did not understand, things too wonderful for me to know. You said, 'Listen now, and I will speak; I will question you, and you shall answer Me.' My ears had heard of You but now my eyes have seen You. THERE-FORE I DESPISE MYSELF AND REPENT IN DUST AND ASHES."
>
> Job 42:1-6

God is wooing us to Himself. He wants to deliver us.

If Job never sinned, then why would he repent? There would be no need for him to repent if there was no sin in his life. Job repented because there *was* sin there and he finally came to admit it and ask God to forgive him for it.

"S U R E L Y   I   S P O K E   O F   T H I N G S
I   D I D   N O T   U N D E R S T A N D"

There was not only sin, but we can *see* from what Job said throughout this book, and especially what he said in this passage of Scripture, that there was a "lack of knowledge." Job spoke many things that were wrong about God because of his lack of knowledge. He did not have a clear understanding of God—especially about God's heart toward him. The Bible says that "My people PERISH because of A LACK OF KNOWLEDGE" (Hosea 4:6). There it is. There is a third explanation as to how the enemy got in there to do what he did to Job!

So, there was sin, fear, and a lack of knowledge. There may have been other things as well. The important thing to know is that it was *not God just deciding one day that all these bad things should happen to this man Job*! It was not God just deciding to test Job to show Satan what Job was made of. Doing something like that was not in God's heart for Job, nor for any of us! God loves us. He is 100 percent for us all the time!

Our enemy the devil is the one who is against us! He is not just our enemy but also God's enemy as well! God opposes him, especially when he tries to harm one of His children. He does not work hand-in-hand with the enemy! It is very clear from the beginning who these tragedies were from. They were not from God but rather from the enemy. They were not from God's hand, but from Satan's hand.

S H O W   M E   Y O U R   H E A R T   I N   T H I S   B O O K

As I studied Job, I pleaded with God, "Please show me Your heart in this book—show me Your heart for this man Job." Soon after I prayed, I saw it! God led me to something Elihu said to Job:

He [God] is WOOING you from the jaws of distress to a
RIGHTEOUS PLACE FREE FROM RESTRICTION,
TO THE COMFORT OF YOUR TABLE LADEN
WITH CHOICE FOOD.

Job 36:16

There it is! There is God's heart for Job and for all of us whenever we are in sin and we have gotten ourselves into a mess. He is "wooing" us to repent so that He can be able to pour out His blessings to us again! God hates sin because it can prevent Him from giving us all that He desires. God wants to "lift *us* out of the slimy pit, out of the mud and mire; and set *our* feet on a rock and give *us* a firm place to stand" (Psalm 40:2). God wants to bring us into a "RIGHTEOUS place FREE from restriction, to the COMFORT of His table laden with CHOICE food"!

God was "wooing" Job while he was suffering from the things Satan had done to him. Elihu told Job how God would chasten him or correct him *while* he was sick or "in affliction" (Job 36:15). God speaks to us *during* times like this also! Thank God that He does and that He truly "NEVER leaves us nor forsakes us!" He speaks to us *during* times when Satan has gotten a foothold in our lives in order to lead us out of the mess. God speaks to us *while* we are in the pit in order to get us out of the pit! The Bible says that His "kindness leads us toward repentance." It is His steadfast and enduring love for us that leads us back to Him during these times.

Elihu says what happens when someone repents of their sin:

His flesh is RENEWED like a child's; it is RESTORED as
in the days of his youth. He prays to God and finds favor
with him, he sees God's face [who God REALLY is and
His very heart] and SHOUTS FOR JOY; he is
RESTORED BY GOD to his RIGHTEOUS STATE.
    Then he comes to men and says, "I sinned, and per-
verted what was right, BUT I DID NOT GET WHAT I

DESERVED [instead, I received MERCY]. He redeemed
my soul from going down to the pit, and I will LIVE TO
ENJOY THE LIGHT!"

Job 33:25-28

That's just what God did at the end of the book! God is so
awesome! God was able to lift Job out of the pit. After Job
repented, God was then able to give him ALL of the blessings
that he wanted for him. Job "shouted for joy," was "returned to his
righteous state," was "redeemed from going down to the pit," and
he "lived to enjoy the light!"

God "BLESSED the latter part of Job's life more than the
first. He had FOURTEEN THOUSAND sheep, SIX
THOUSAND camels, a THOUSAND yoke of oxen and
a THOUSAND donkeys. And he also had SEVEN sons

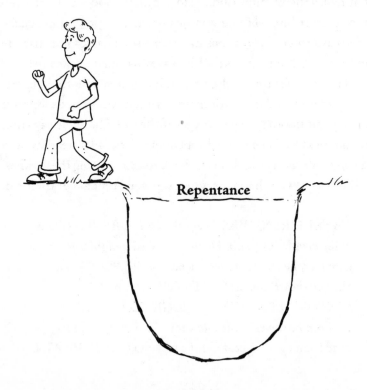

Repentance

and THREE daughters...Nowhere in all the land were
there found women as BEAUTIFUL as Job's daughters,
and their father granted them an INHERITANCE along
with their brothers. After this, Job lived a HUNDRED
AND FORTY YEARS [a "long" and "satisfying" life—
smile]; he saw his children and their children to the
FOURTH GENERATION!"

Job 42:12,13,15,16

That was the heart of God, to bless Job with these things.
He was unable to do that until Job repented. *Then* God poured
out "abundant life" on him!

HOW DID THE HEDGE OF PROTECTION GET BROKEN?

One of the main reasons why I got confused about this book
was because I did not understand about the "hedge of protection" that God had made around Job. I did not understand the
extent of this hedge or how it got there. It just says that God had
made this hedge of protection around Job.

First, I needed to understand that the book of Job was one of
the oldest books of the Bible. It was written before Moses and
the law and before Jesus, who "redeemed us from the curse of the
law" and gave us "authority over the enemy." Things were much
different during this time than they are today. Job did not have
the same covenant with God that we are privileged to have. We
have a blood covenant through God's Son Jesus, and we receive
from God by grace through our faith. Also, there was not a lot of
revelation about who God was since they did not have the Word
of God as we have it today. Job did not have the Holy Spirit living inside him as we do. He did not have the inner strength we
are privileged to have.

God was able to build a "hedge" around Job primarily
because of Job's *obedience*. God was not able to put this hedge

around others who were in disobedience. Just because there was a hedge around Job, and God referred to him as "blameless and upright, a man who fears God and shuns evil" (Job 1:1,8; 2:3), it did *not* mean that he was without sin! No man is without sin— not one of us is perfect.

The word *perfect* (KJV) simply means that Job was a very good man who followed God. If Job was without sin, he would have been just like Jesus! The Bible says that "ALL have sinned and fall short of the glory of God" (Romans 3:23) and that included Job. We can think of the greatest Christian we know and realize that even that person is not without sin in their lives. Even Paul acknowledged sin in his life, and he truly was one of the greatest Christians ever.

Because there was sin in Job's life, there was an opening in that hedge. Satan knew that. Satan is no dummy! The Bible calls him the "accuser of our brothers" (Revelation 12:10). That's just what he was doing that day when he talked to God about Job. He was accusing Job of his sin before God.

God knows all things! He even knew Job's heart. Satan was not telling God anything that He did not already know. Satan did not trick God! It would be *impossible* for Satan to be able to do that. God is omnipotent and Satan is just a fallen angel.

The bottom line is that Satan had a legal right to hurt Job. God knew that. Who gave Satan a legal right to have the power he has in the world? *Man* did when Adam and Eve sinned! Satan was given the legal right to do these things when man bowed to him in the garden. Satan *knew* that "everything that Job had was in his hands" (Job 1:12). God was not *giving* Satan permission to do harm to Job, rather He was referring to the fact that unfortunately, Satan *had* a legal right to do that!

I asked God about this hedge and how He was able to limit what Satan was able to do to Job. Satan's mission is to "kill, steal and destroy," and if he could have, we know that Satan would have killed Job on the spot! But Satan could not do that! Why?

God showed me that the hedge of protection was broken because of fear, sin, and a lack of knowledge. The hedge had a *gap* in it where Satan could get in. That gap was big enough for Satan to get in to destroy all that Job had, but he could not hurt Job, at least not at first.

What happened after the first calamity? Job never looked inside himself nor did he repent of any wrongdoing. Therefore, the hedge of protection was broken farther, the gap was bigger, and *then* Satan was able to actually hurt his body. Job went deeper down into this pit. Still, at this time, the hedge was not completely gone because Satan could not kill him, which is what he really wanted to do!

What would have happened if Job had continued in sin and not repented? We can read about what would have eventually happened to Job in what Elihu said:

> *The godless in heart harbor resentment; even when He fetters them, they do not cry for help. They DIE IN THEIR YOUTH, among male prostitutes of the shrines.*
>
> Job 36:13,14

Also Elihu said:

> *He [God] may speak in their ears and terrify them with warnings, to TURN A MAN FROM WRONGDOING and keep him from PRIDE, to PRESERVE HIS SOUL FROM THE PIT, HIS LIFE FROM PERISHING BY THE SWORD.*
>
> Job 33:13-18

So, if Job had not repented, he would have died! He would have continued to sink farther and farther down into this pit. What was God doing all of this time? God was "wooing" him, trying to "turn him from wrongdoing." God was speaking to him in order to save him out of that pit. God did not want Job to die but rather to live! Thank God that this story has a happy ending and Job did indeed repent and live!

I asked God what would have happened if Job had repented after the first calamity hit his life. Job did not repent after this, but held onto his "integrity," which is the belief that he had done nothing wrong. Then he made an erroneous statement in saying that the "Lord gives and the Lord takes away." He blamed God for causing this calamity when it was *Satan* who did all of this! (It is amazing how many people quote that verse as if they are quoting something that is pleasing to God, when in fact it is not.)

God showed me that if Job had repented of sin, that the second calamity never would have been able to happen! Satan would not have been able to touch him. That hedge of protection would have been restored, and Satan would not have been able to hurt Job at all!

If only after the first calamity, Job had prayed as David prayed:

SEARCH ME, O God, and KNOW MY HEART; test me and know my anxious thoughts. SEE if there is any OFFEN-SIVE WAY IN ME, and lead me in the way everlasting.
Psalm 139:23,24

David prayed and asked God to look inside him and show him if there was any sin in his life. He asked God to help him to judge himself. He desired for God to show him if any of his actions, his words, or his heart were "offensive" to Him. Then He asked God to lead him in His ways, which are good and "everlasting." David was open to hearing rebuke and correction from God and was not just open to it, he was *looking* for it! He wanted to make sure there was no sin in his life and that he was living in a way that pleased God as he wrote this psalm.

If Job had prayed a prayer like that, God would have been able to show him where there was sin, where there was fear, and would have been able to give him the knowledge he needed to restore that hedge of protection around him. That takes a certain amount of humbleness toward God to pray like this. It takes admitting that you are not perfect and that you need God to help you to not just see the sin in your life but also to deal with it effectively. If only Job had done that.

Job Held Onto His Integrity
The Belief That He
Did Nothing Wrong

After God showed me all of this, there was still a verse that continued to confuse me:

> God said, "And he [Job] still maintains his integrity, though you [Satan] incited Me against him to ruin him without any reason."
>
> Job 2:3

I asked God about this because it sounded like Satan tricked God into doing something that was wrong. But we know that Satan is *incapable* of doing that. God knows *far more* than Satan. So, that cannot be the correct interpretation of that verse.

Then I thought, it sounded like Satan coerced God into doing something that was wrong, which is sin! We know that this cannot be correct because God is perfect, holy, and has no sin! God is incapable of doing wrong! As Elihu said:

> FAR BE IT from God to do EVIL, for the Almighty to do WRONG. He repays a man for what he has DONE; He brings upon him what HIS CONDUCT DESERVES. It is UNTHINKABLE that God would do WRONG, that the Almighty would PERVERT JUSTICE!
>
> Job 34:10-12

So, what is the correct interpretation of this verse? God pointed out the fact that it was Job who kept mentioning his "integrity." The word *integrity* was used by Job several times in this book to describe what he was doing. This verse describes what Job was doing and how Job felt. In other words, God was saying, "And Job still maintains his integrity or rather he still insists that he has no sin in his life, even though he [Job] thinks that Satan incited Me to ruin him without reason." God was not describing what *actually happened* but rather how Job was perceiving what had happened! Praise God for His Holy Spirit who "teaches us all things" and "leads us into all truth"! The Holy Spirit opens our eyes to God's truth so that we can *see* things correctly and know His very heart for us!

There's one more verse at the end of this book that also confused me:

> *After Job had prayed for his friends, the Lord made him prosperous again and gave him twice as much as he had before. All his brothers and sisters and everyone who had known him before came and ate with him in his house. They comforted and consoled him over ALL THE TROUBLE THE LORD HAD BROUGHT UPON HIM, and each one gave him a piece of silver and a gold ring.*
>
> Job 42:10,11

This verse again sounded like it was God who brought this "trouble" upon Job. But it is clear from the beginning that it was *not* God who did this, but rather Satan. God did not cause these calamities to happen to Job, Satan did. God showed me that this verse refers to how the people viewed what had happened to Job and not what actually happened. Job was not alone in his misinterpretation of God during this time. These people did not have the Word of God to tell them what God was like. Also, during this time period, they had little or no knowledge of Satan, so God was essentially blamed for everything that happened to them!

So, Job is actually a great book about the mercy and love of God for a wonderful man named Job. God will help us to find His heart in every page of His Word, as well as every *page of our lives* as we seek Him.

GOD'S HEART IN THE OLD TESTAMENT

I often wondered why Satan was not mentioned much in the Old Testament. Not much is said and there appears to be very little knowledge of him by the people who lived back then. Why is that?

In the New Testament, Jesus did a substantial amount of teaching about the enemy. He even taught how we are to resist him and stand against him with the Word of God. The Bible says that we are not to be "unaware of his schemes" (2 Corinthians 2:11). Jesus made it very clear what things were from Satan and what things were from God.

AUTHORITY OVER THE ENEMY

God showed me that one reason for this was because Jesus gave us authority over Satan. Since the death and resurrection of Jesus, things changed. We received power and authority over the enemy because Jesus defeated him for us when he rose again! It was at that time that Satan was put in his place, which is under our feet!

What about the people in the Old Testament? People did *not* have authority over Satan. God protected the people but it was based on their obedience to Him. The average person could not take authority over the enemy. There were prophets of God who were anointed to defeat the enemy, but the average person did not walk in this power. The Holy Spirit was not given to us until the day of Pentecost, after Jesus rose again.

So, why don't we hear much about Satan in the Old Testament? We read about him in Genesis, a little in Job and a little here and there. Where was he? Did he take a vacation during all of this time? I don't think so! Unfortunately he was alive and well, doing what he does best, which is "killing, stealing and destroying"!

I believe that one reason people did not know a lot about Satan is because God did not want them to focus on him. Why? Because they were not *equipped* to deal with him. What kept them safe was their relationship with God—their obedience to Him. God knew what was best for the people back then, and that was best. However, the price that was paid was that God often got blamed for many of the calamities that happened.

WHAT IS GOD'S HEART?

In many of the accounts of the Old Testament, it is unclear who was causing the destruction, God or Satan! Sometimes it appeared to be God and the result of His wrath. People got into sin and continued in it without repenting, and destruction came. Examples of these are the flood in the time of Noah and the city of Sodom and Gomorrah in the time of Lot. God's wrath comes automatically because of sin—it is a spiritual law. Just as an apple will fall to the ground because of the law of gravity, God's wrath will come as a result of unrepentant sin. The Bible says that people will "reap" what they sow (Galatians 6:7,8).

As I was writing this book, I asked God, "How do I explain this?" Instead of going through each and every account of the Old Testament to decipher who was causing the calamity, why it happened, and where God was in it, He told me that as far as this book was concerned, it didn't matter. What He wanted me to focus on was knowing and trusting His heart.

First, God wanted me to explain that if bad things happened in the Bible where God or Satan are mentioned in doing something destructive, we can *know* that there was indeed *sin* involved. God is a just and a fair God. Things just did not happen without a reason. Sin would open the door for Satan to hurt them, or it would result in the wrath of God.

Second, God wanted me to focus on what was in His heart toward His people. It didn't matter if it was God's wrath or Satan that caused the calamity because His heart was the same. If those people were hurting, He also ached, grieved, and was hurt as well! He is a God of compassion! He is the "same yesterday and today and forever" (Hebrews 13:8). He is a God who feels it when we hurt and He is "touched with the feeling of our infirmities" (Hebrews 4:15; KJV). The Bible clearly says that He takes no pleasure when people are hurting, whether it be during times of His wrath when they are in sin, or in times when it is Satan who is attacking them. He hurts either way!

If it is during His wrath, the Bible talks about God's heart and how He is full of compassion and an unfailing love. God *spoke* this word to me one time, "*My heart is outside of My wrath.*" We can *see* that in these verses that reveal His reluctance even when His wrath occurs:

> For men are not cast off by the Lord forever. Though He brings grief, He will show COMPASSION, so great is HIS UNFAILING LOVE. For He does not WILLINGLY bring affliction or grief to the children of men.
>
> Lamentations 3:31-33

*"As surely as I live," declares the Sovereign Lord, "I take
NO PLEASURE in the death of the wicked, but rather
that they TURN FROM THEIR WAYS AND LIVE."*
Ezekiel 33:11

God was reluctant to send His wrath upon those who continued to worship idols and live in immorality in the Old
Testament. He wanted to establish a way that people could
escape that wrath. So, what did He do? In the New Testament,
we find this exciting verse:

*Since we have now been justified by His blood, how much
more shall we be SAVED from GOD'S WRATH through
HIM!*
Romans 5:9

God sent Jesus to "save" us from that wrath! Praise Him!
So, what is God's heart if it is Satan who is hurting the
people? God says:

*If anyone does attack you, it will NOT be My doing; who-
ever attacks you will surrender to you.*
Isaiah 54:15

So, God's heart is the same in either circumstance. His heart
is not in His wrath, nor is His heart in anything that the enemy
did to the people. If they hurt, He hurts! He is a God of compassion and love!

Another thing that was recently discovered is that the verb
that means "to cause" can actually be interpreted as "to allow."
Many of the stories in the Bible refer to God *causing* bad things
to happen, when in fact, they really meant that God *allowed* these
things to happen because *He allowed man to sin.* It was not in the
sense that God *chose* to allow these things to happen because it

was simply His will, but that He *had* to because of their sin! These things were allowed to happen because man was given a free will that allowed him to sin and therefore to reap the consequences that followed.

FOR THE SAKE OF THE ELECT

God showed me some other things about the Old Testament. I used to read the stories about how whole cities were wiped out and how people were killed for their sins. It all seemed so harsh to me, and I wondered how a loving God could ever command things like that to be done. God showed me that these things were actually done out of His *love* for His people in an attempt to keep them clean and pure, and therefore *safe*! He showed me that these things were done for the sake of the "elect" (Isaiah 45:4, Matthew 24:31 and other verses) and to preserve His "seed" (Genesis 13:16, Galatians 3:29 and other verses).

First, God does not handpick people today to be Christians and saved. No, He offers salvation to every single person. He loves us all the same! The "elect" just means that He knows ahead of time who will be saved. God knows everything, including the future. We all have a free will to choose Him or not, but He knows who will do so.

We see God working throughout all the generations—from Abraham, to Noah, to Moses, to David, through the Jews, etc., to Jesus, to the disciples, to Paul, to the Gentiles, to you and to me! All that was done was actually done for *us*! He did it to *ensure* that we would be able to have a relationship with Him and therefore be His true sons and daughters!

What was it like back then? The Bible tells us of His people who were trying to follow Him. It also talks about others who were worshipping idols, those who were wicked, and people who were actually enemies of His people and therefore out to destroy them. The wicked were often destroyed in order to keep His people safe and alive!

To Preserve His Seed

People were also destroyed to keep His people holy, which would also keep them safe. Sin led to destruction. Sinfulness had a way of rubbing off on His people, even as it does today. Back then, it was vital that people live in obedience to God because their protection was based on this. In all of this, God was *preserving* His people so that His people would not only survive, but also multiply.

When reading about these accounts, we need to keep in mind who God is. We need to remember that God is holy and just and that He is incapable of being unfair. If we read something that seems unfair, then *we* are missing something. God knows people's hearts. He knows if people will be repentant or if their hearts are hardened and opposed to Him and will therefore never repent.

We need to remember not only who God is, but especially His heart. God takes no pleasure in seeing people hurt or in seeing people suffer and die. What He did in protecting His people was not only for His people back then, but also for us! It is so awesome to see the result of all that He did during that time and how it affects everything today. What started off as a handful of people is now a multitude—thousands and thousands, even million of Christians today! God's desire was to have true sons and daughters who would love Him just because they chose to love Him, and look at how large His family is now!

A DAY GOD WEPT

*G*od hurts when we hurt, and on September 11, 2001, God wept. On that day, about three thousand innocent people were killed as terrorists flew planes into buildings in this country. Afterward, many people asked, "Where was God?" Many blamed God. Many felt like this was God's judgment on the United States. Some felt that it had nothing at all to do with God, but it was just about some evil men who did an evil thing.

I watched the terrible events over and over again as I worked at the hospital that day. I felt bad for the thousands of people who lost their lives and were injured. I felt awful for those who lost loved ones and I hurt for the police and firemen who gave their lives trying to save people. I knew God was hurting as well. He was touched by the infirmities of all these people. His heart was heavy that day and during the many days ahead as people grieved.

I knew it wasn't God who caused this to happen. God loves us with a love that "surpasses knowledge." Satan, however, comes to "kill, steal and destroy" so his fingerprints were all over this! He was the one who put thoughts and plans into the minds of these men and directed them to do these evil things. These men were deceived into believing that they were actually doing something good and honorable for their god. That is the reason Jesus said that Satan "is a liar and the father of it" (John 8:33), because he will work to deceive people to cause them to do his work of destruction.

SEARCH US, OH GOD

I knew that Satan was behind this. I prayed and asked God, "How did he get in to do these terrible things to the people in this country?" This is a great country and there are many Christians who live here and are praying for the United States. What happened to our hedge of protection?

Even though this is truly a wonderful country, I knew that there was still so much wrong with it. I could clearly see the racism, the abortion, the immorality, the crimes, the pornography, the injustice, the foul language, etc. All I had to do was turn on the TV to see the crime on the news, or see the immorality on the sit-coms, or listen to the foul language on the talk shows, and it was clear that there was still *much* that was wrong! I could see it not just in those who were not Christian, but I could also see it in some Christians who were either in sin or just apathetic to what was going on.

As I sought God about this, He impressed upon me to repent. So as a citizen, I repented for the sins of the nation—my nation. One of the first things I do if I sense an attack by the enemy is look inside myself. I examine myself to see if there is any area of my life where I have given the enemy a foothold. I prayed for forgiveness for this nation as God showed me things to pray about, for Christians and non-Christians. A popular verse in the Bible which talks about Christians repenting for the sake of their country. It is a beautiful promise from God:

If My people, who are called by My name, will humble themselves and pray and seek My face and turn from their wicked ways, then will I HEAR FROM HEAVEN and will FORGIVE THEIR SIN and will HEAL THEIR LAND.

2 Chronicles 7:14-16

I know that many other Christians heard the same thing from God and started to pray. I knew that acknowledging our sin, repenting, and receiving forgiveness would restore that hedge of protection.

Help Us to Not Make the Same Mistake As Job

God brought to mind the story of Job. I thought about the fact that if he had only looked within himself after the first tragedy happened and repented, then the second tragedy would never have happened. Repentance would have plugged up the hole in his hedge of protection. I didn't want another tragedy to happen as it did in Job's life.

As I looked around and as I listened to the media, I became a little concerned about what I saw happening in the country. People everywhere took on a new sense of national *pride*. People were saying that they were proud to be American and proud of their country. They were saying all kinds of good things about this country. Many even implied that this country was indeed so great that there was no *reason* for something bad to ever happen here!

I deeply love this country and I would not choose to live anywhere else. I was happy with the fact that Americans were proud of this country instead of putting this great country down. However, I did not want us to get into the *sin* of pride. I prayed that people would look within and repent of where this country was wrong. Even though this country is so great, I did not want people to hold onto their "integrity" as Job did and believe that there was nothing at all wrong in this nation.

It has been a few years now, and we have been blessed since that day in September. We have had no more major tragedies. Praise God. I feel as if repentance is an ongoing thing that we need to continue to do, even as we do in our personal lives. It is always important to look inside and repent of the things that we do wrong on an on-going basis. We need to remain sensitive to the Holy Spirit when He shows us things that are wrong in our lives, as well as in our nation. Repentance is one of the number one things that keeps our hedge of protection safe and strong.

What about all of the people who died in this tragedy? I was very relieved that not more died. I remembered the estimates that had been given when it first happened. They were initially predicting around twenty thousand people in *each* building! The toll for the two towers actually turned out to be under three thousand. Even one person dying is one too many as far as God is concerned, but under three thousand is far better than forty thousand people!

God Was Busy That Day Working for Each and Every Person

What about all of these people? I have heard numerous stories about how God worked to either prevent people from going to those buildings that day or worked to help them to escape. God was indeed working 100 percent of the time in each and every person's life to save them! If we come to the conclusion that He only helped a chosen few, then we make Him out to be a "respecter of persons" and therefore loving and caring about some more than others. We know that God is not at all like that. He is "NO respecter of persons" and loves and cares for each one of us the same!

So, if it was His will to help everyone that day, what happened to those who did not make it out alive? I believe that He was trying to warn *everyone*, which is what was in His heart! Some people were able to *hear* Him while others unfortunately were not, for whatever reason. The Bible says that God speaks to us in a "still small voice" (1 Kings 19:12). I'm sure that many of the people who perished were not Christian and were probably unable to hear His voice. I wondered though about the Christians who died. Were they so busy or so involved in their responsibilities and what they *thought* was the right thing to do that day that they ignored any hint about not going to the office? Maybe there were some Christians who had gone astray or some who were just not walking close to God that day and missed hearing Him. Maybe there were some who were new Christians and had not been used to hearing His voice. Whatever the case, I know that God was very busy that day doing *all that He could do* to keep people off those planes and out of those buildings. He is always 100 percent for us, 100 percent of the time! He is always at work on our behalf because He loves us.

WOULD I HAVE HEARD YOU, LORD?

I feel so bad for those who were killed that day. I have often wondered if I would have hearkened to God's voice. I have wondered if I would have heard His "still small voice" telling me to not go to work. Would I have done that? Would I have known it was God or thought that I was just imagining it. Would I have assumed that I should go to work because that is what I did every day? Would I have been able to even entertain the thought of staying home or doing something different?

Since that day, God has impressed upon me the importance of not *assuming* anything! God has shown me the importance of praying about everything I do and seeking His guidance in it, instead of just *assuming* that I know what His will is each day. In the morning when I get up, I ask God what He wants me to do. I am now more prepared to hear something that is not my normal routine. I am even ready to hear God tell me to not go to work if that is what He wants from me. I am more concerned about what He thinks of me than what my boss thinks of me. I am not in any way being disrespectful because God wants us to work as unto Him in our jobs and to always do a good job. However, if there is ever a time when He tells us to do something different than our boss tells us to do, we need to always put Him first, not our boss.

What about all of the firemen and policemen who gave their lives for the people inside those buildings? They are to be commended. They went to their jobs that day—jobs that they knew beforehand were jobs that would help people but also possibly put themselves in danger. People are to be commended for choosing such professions, for they are looking out for the welfare of other people even *above* their own welfare. The Bible says that there is "no greater love" than when someone "lays down his life for his friend" (John 15:13). They were serving God and serving others on that day when they rushed into those buildings. They were doing the Father's heart, which was reaching out to save those people.

Being "Filled to the Measure" with God!

With two children at home, we have watched almost every Disney movie ever made. One of my favorites is *The Lion King*. The movie is about a lion named Simba. His father, who is the king, is killed and Simba is to be heir to the throne. Instead of taking his place as king, he runs away and hides. He eventually gets used to his new life and forgets who he really is.

One day, while looking at his reflection in the water, Simba sees his face gradually change into his *father's* face. As he looks into his eyes, he actually sees his *father's* eyes looking back at him! He even hears his *father's* voice! He is then reminded of who he really is, that he is *really a king*! After seeing his father's face, he bravely gets up and returns to his home to live the life of a king.

I always cry when it gets to that part of the movie. It is such a tender moment between a father and his son, Simba. The movie speaks to me of how I need to be reminded of who I really am and *Who* lives within me! Every day I want to be "filled to the measure of all the fullness of God" and let Him live through me in all of that fullness! I want to be able to look in the mirror each morning and be reminded that I have a big God who lives within me. I want all of His power, love, peace, wisdom, and knowledge to flow through me to touch the people around me and change the world.

How do we as Christians get to the point where we are "filled to the measure of all the fullness of God"? How do we do that? In Ephesians 3:16-19, God tells us that it is actually based on how well we *know His love*!

OUR LOVE FOR GOD

One of the greatest things that happens as we understand and experience God's love in our lives is that *our love for Him grows*! As we taste of God's love, our hearts are touched by His heart and they are *changed*.

Loving God is so important. If we could talk face-to-face with God and ask Him what He wanted most from us, He would

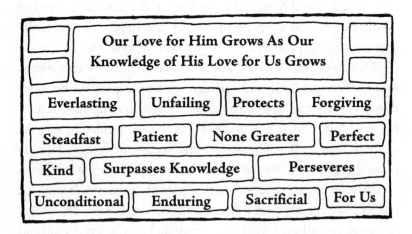

Our Love for Him Grows As Our Knowledge of His Love for Us Grows

Everlasting	Unfailing	Protects	Forgiving
Steadfast	Patient	None Greater	Perfect
Kind	Surpasses Knowledge		Perseveres
Unconditional	Enduring	Sacrificial	For Us

say…"To love Me." Loving Him first in our lives is the "greatest commandment"—it is what God desires *most* from each one of us:

> Hearing that Jesus had silenced the Sadducees, the
> Pharisees got together. One of them, an expert in the law,
> tested Him with this question: "Teacher, which is the
> GREATEST commandment in the Law?"
> Jesus replied: "Love the Lord your God with ALL your
> heart and with ALL your soul and with ALL your mind.
> This is the FIRST and GREATEST commandment."
>
> Matthew 22:34-38

Isn't that awesome that the God of the universe, the Almighty God, the Creator of Heaven and Earth, desires you and me to love Him! That is what is most important to Him, *our love!* It amazes me that He would want to have a relationship with us—with you and me! Who are we that He, the Almighty God, should feel this way about us? As the Bible says:

> When I consider Your heavens, the work of Your fingers,
> the moon and the stars, which You have set in place, what
> is MAN that you are mindful of him, the son of man that
> you care for HIM?
>
> Psalm 8:3,4

God loves us so much and the *most important* thing to Him is for us to love Him! He is able to work in our hearts as we come to know His great love for us. He can change our hearts!

> The Lord your God will CIRCUMCISE YOUR HEART
> and the hearts of your descendants, so that you may LOVE
> HIM with ALL your heart and with ALL your soul, and
> live.
>
> Deuteronomy 30:6

*I will give them an UNDIVIDED HEART and put a
new spirit in them; I will remove from them their heart of
stone and give them a HEART OF FLESH.*

Ezekiel 11:19,20

*I will give them a HEART TO KNOW ME, that I am
the Lord. They will be My people, and I will be their God,
for they will return to Me with ALL of their heart.*

Jeremiah 24:7

OBEDIENCE

As we grow to know God's love, our love for Him grows.
Then something ELSE begins to happen! We start to see our
lives change—the way we think, feel, and the things we do! We
find that we *want* to please God—we find ourselves loving the
things that He loves more and more and not wanting to do those
things that would hurt Him.

OBEDIENCE

OUR LOVE FOR GOD

KNOWING GOD'S LOVE

If you love Me, you will obey what I command.

John 14:15

The more we love God, the more we *want* to follow Him, the more we *want* to please Him, the more we *want* to obey Him. Jesus is our best example of this. He knew the Father's love for Him and because of this He went around "always doing what pleased Him" (John 8:29). He even called doing this His "food" (John 4:34).

Knowing how much God loves us causes a change in our hearts and a desire to live for Him:

For Christ's love COMPELS US, because we are convinced that one died for all, and therefore all died. And He died for all, that those who live should no longer live for themselves but FOR HIM who died for them and was raised again.

2 Corinthians 5:14,15

God wants us to obey Him, but He doesn't want us to do this grudgingly or under compulsion, but rather out of our love for Him! He wants us to love Him so much that we will *want* to follow Him in our lives.

God is so awesome that He actually can work in our hearts to help us to want to follow Him!

For it is God who works in you to WILL and to ACT according to His good purpose.

Philippians 2:13

Restore to me the joy of Your salvation and grant me a WILLING SPIRIT, to sustain me.

Psalm 51:12

A SURRENDERED LIFE

As we grow to know God's love more and more, we not only love Him more, but we also *trust* Him more. We can trust

Someone who loves us with a love that "surpasses knowledge"! We know that whatever He wants to do in our lives is good and that He desires the best for us. As we know God's love for us there is actually a *surrendering* that takes place. We open ourselves up to God to let Him have *His* way in our lives.

In this day and age, many people do not like that word *surrender*. It hints at not having control or implies that you can be taken advantage of, or that you are somehow weak or inferior. That is *far* from how God looks at a life that is completely surrendered to Him. In fact a surrendered life actually implies a *powerful* life! A surrendered life is really one in which a person can walk in the fullness of God's love and the fullness of God's power with signs and wonders following him even as they did in the life of Jesus. Jesus was surrendered to God and look at all that He did! In fact Jesus said:

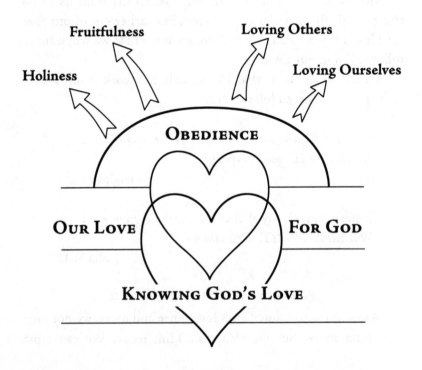

I tell you the truth, anyone who has faith in Me will do
what I have been doing. He will do even GREATER things
than these, because I am going to the Father.

John 14:12

What happens when we surrender our lives to Him? God is able to work in and through us. As we surrender one area, He is able to work there; as we surrender another area, He is able to work there as well…and so on. He comes into these areas— changing us, molding us, making us better and filling us with His presence and power! He literally fills us with Himself and His life-changing power and we are "transformed into His likeness with ever-increasing glory"! (2 Corinthians 3:18).

CHRIST MANIFESTING HIMSELF
THROUGH ME

God helped me to understand this better by using the example of a multivitamin. All of the minerals and vitamins you need are in that multivitamin. It is quite small and in a concentrated capsule, but everything is in there. When we first became Christians, God gave us the Holy Spirit. The Bible says that we were "marked in Him with a seal, the promised Holy Spirit" (Ephesians 1:13). It even says that "if anyone does not have the Spirit of Christ, he does not belong to Christ" (Romans 8:9).

Jesus came to live within us through His Holy Spirit! ALL of His power, love, strength, peace, and wisdom came inside each one of us! He showed me that His Holy Spirit is like that strong multivitamin. Everything is within us but in a concentrated capsule form. Just as all of the vitamins and minerals are in that vitamin, all of JESUS is in us through His Holy Spirit. We are not just given *part* of Him, but we are given *all* of Him. He does not give one person some of Himself and another person a different piece of Himself. No, all of Him is in each one of us. We all have the *same* Holy Spirit!

Even so, the Lord does not want to STAY like that in that small, concentrated capsule form. It is His desire to *permeate* our lives and to *manifest* Himself through us! He wants to fill us and live through us. He wants to spread out within us so that His feet can walk through our feet, His mouth can speak through our mouths, His hands can touch people through our hands, and His heart can be moved with compassion through our hearts. As we surrender our lives to Him and stand by faith, He is actually able to manifest Himself through us! We are, in other words, able to tap into Him and all that He has within us. We are able to draw upon His power in order to do the great things that He did and now desires to do through us.

God is so good. He is a God of great integrity and honor. He will never force His will on us, even though His will is the best plan for our lives. He will never go against our will. Instead, He is a God who waits on *us* to ask Him to fill us. He waits until *we* surrender our lives to Him.

There are exciting verses in the Bible that explain what happens as we open our lives up to God:

> *For those God foreknew He also predestined to be CON-FORMED TO THE LIKENESS OF HIS SON, that He might be the firstborn among many brothers.*
>
> Romans 8:29

Paul stated that He wished for the Christians in Ephesus to "become MATURE, attaining to the WHOLE MEASURE OF THE FULLNESS OF CHRIST" (Ephesians 4:13).

Peter gave reference that we can "PARTICIPATE in the DIVINE NATURE" (2 Peter 1:4).

And I LOVE this verse:

In this way, LOVE is made COMPLETE among us so
that we will have confidence on the day of judgment,
because IN THIS WORLD WE ARE LIKE HIM.

1 John 4:17

All of these verses talk about a wonderful change that takes
place in us as Christians as we grow in our relationship with the
Lord. However, in order to grow in our relationship with Him,
we need to grow in knowing His great love for us. *That* is the
foundation upon which *everything* else is built! As that foundation grows *brick by brick*, our love for Him grows. As our love for
Him grows, our desire to please Him grows. We actually become
more like Him—which is our goal. He is able to *manifest* His
character through us—His strength, His peace, His wisdom,
His power, everything! Praise God! Paul profoundly said:

I no longer live, but CHRIST lives in ME.

Galatians 2:20

How Does JESUS Feel about This?

It is so awesome to think about being able to have Jesus living within us! But, have you ever thought about how He must feel? Have you ever thought about how He feels in regard to being able to live through us by the power of His Holy Spirit?

When Jesus left to go back to the Father after His resurrection, He had to leave the disciples, His family, and all the people who He deeply loved. Instead of just leaving and not being able to be with them until they went to Heaven, He had the expectation of living within those who followed Him through His Holy Spirit! He knew that He truly would "never leave them nor forsake them"! He knew that He would be with them always and forever!

One morning the Lord gave me a glimpse of His heart concerning this. I was slowly waking up, still a little groggy, and I heard Him *say* with anticipation, "Hurry up, wake up! I have so much I want to do with you today!" It was neat to sense not only how much He loved being with me, but also how much He loved living through me—how He could still reach out and touch so many people, through *me*! He loves living through us! He truly does touch people through our hands and speak to them through our voices. His ministry continues on through us for we are truly the "body of Christ" (1 Corinthians 12:27).

Being "Filled to the Measure" with Love!

$\mathcal{B}$eing filled to the measure of all the fullness of God *has* to include God's love. How could we even imagine being filled with Him without being filled with His love? It would be impossible! For the Bible says:

> God IS love. Whoever lives in love lives in God, and God lives in him.
>
> 1 John 4:16

There are verses in the Bible that tell us that as Christians, God's love is already inside of us:

> God has poured out HIS LOVE into OUR HEARTS by the Holy Spirit.
>
> Romans 5:5

> Jesus also prayed, "I have made You known to them, and will continue to make You known in order that the LOVE

YOU HAVE FOR ME MAY BE IN THEM *and that I*
MYSELF MAY BE IN THEM!"

John 17:26

Therefore, we have God's love already inside us, to love Him with and other people with! Even though His love is within us, it is not *manifested* in our lives until we come to know His love and walk in it.

God commands us to love one another and to walk in love. Our lives as Christians should be characterized by love, even as Christ's life was. God wants us to be "vessels for noble purposes" (2 Timothy 2:21), through whom His love flows abundantly to others.

What if we hold unforgiveness, offense, anger, bitterness, jealousy, envy, or hatred in our hearts? Unfortunately, the love of God is not able to flow through us as it should. It's as if the channel of His love gets *plugged up*, like a drain pipe that gets full of all kinds of stuff that shouldn't be there. As we deal with this "stuff" effectively, through prayer, forgiveness, and the power of His Word, God's love is able to flow through us again.

God wants to live through us! He wants to touch peoples' lives and hearts through us! God wants to love people through you and me!

WE ARE
"LOVE LETTERS"

*W*hen I went away to college, I met a special man and we began to date. However, after spending two years there, I had to transfer to another college to finish my education to become a physical therapist since this college did not offer it. It was sad to say good-bye to him, but we kept in contact through telephone calls and letters.

How I looked forward to getting those letters and cards! They were full of his love and how much he missed me. They were full of words that expressed what was in his heart for me. I think most of us can relate to how nice it is to receive a love letter!

At the beginning of this book I mentioned that this would be a letter of love to you from the Lord. Then as I wrote about Jesus, I said that He *is* God's letter of love to us! He is *the letter of love* that God sent to us: "for God so loved the world that He gave His only Son that whoever believes in Him should not perish but have everlasting life"!

As I was finishing up this book, God led me to some beautiful verses—some verses about you and me!

*This is the covenant I will make with the house of Israel
after that time, declares the Lord. I will put MY LAWS
IN THEIR MINDS and WRITE THEM ON THEIR
HEARTS. I will be their God, and they will be My people.
No longer will a man teach his neighbor or a man his
brother saying, "Know the Lord," because they will all
KNOW ME, from the least of them to the greatest.*

Hebrews 8:10-12

Then Paul wrote this to the Christians at the church of
Corinth:

*You yourselves are our LETTER, written on our
HEARTS, KNOWN and READ BY EVERYBODY. You
show that YOU are a LETTER OF CHRIST, the result of
our ministry, written not with ink but with the SPIRIT
OF THE LIVING GOD, not on tablets of stone but on
tablets of HUMAN HEARTS.*

2 Corinthians 3:2,3

What a beautiful verse about us! That's US!

WE ARE THE "LETTERS OF CHRIST!"

People *read* us and *see* Christ in us! We are full of His love
and full of His power! Actually it's as His *love* flows through us
that His *power* is able to fully flow through us. Jesus was "moved
with compassion....and healed their sick" (Matthew 14:14). He
was *first* moved with love for the people...*then* the power flowed
through Him to bring healing. Jesus wants us to be "moved with
compassion." You might say that He wants us to stay so close to
Him that His heart full of love is manifested through our hearts.
As we *keep in step with His heartbeat,* we are "letters of Christ" to
the rest of the world!!

CHRIST IN US—
"THE HOPE OF GLORY"

*O*ne day as I was driving to work, I just felt exhausted! I had not slept much the night before. As I thought about the long day ahead of me and all the work that I would have to do, I wondered how I was going to get through it!

I prayed about this and asked the Lord to give me strength and energy. He answered me by giving me a *picture* in my mind of a twenty-six-mile marathon runner! I laughed to myself and said, "Lord, I don't need *that* much energy to get through this day!" Then He went a step further and showed me a muscle-bound weight lifter! Again, I laughed and said, "Lord, I don't need *that* much strength to get through this day!" The Lord must have been enjoying this because He went a step further and showed me a thick stone wall that was very high. Then He showed me a tiny ant who was trying to get past the wall. He showed me that this wall was His protection for me against an enemy who is really only the size of an ant! Then I really laughed! I realized that God was showing me that His provision for me was more than enough! His provision was already inside of me! In fact, all that He provided for me was actually *more* than I needed to get through that day.

I continued on to work with a skip in my step, knowing that it was going to be a great day, and that I would indeed get through it. As I hopped into bed that night, I was reminded of how I felt that morning. I was amazed once again by God's love and faithfulness, and to see His awesome power working within me. As I lay there *trying* to fall asleep, I realized that I wasn't even tired, but instead, had energy to spare! (smile)

Jesus said,

> *I tell you the truth, ANYONE who has FAITH in Me will do what I have been doing. He will do EVEN GREATER THINGS THAN THESE, because I am going to the Father.*
>
> John 14:12

I have read about the great men and women in the Bible: Moses, Joshua, Ruth, Paul, and Peter, etc. They are such an inspiration to me—to read how God did such powerful and miraculous things through these people. They were really ordinary people like us who knew God and walked in the fullness of His love and therefore the fullness of His power. I have enjoyed hearing about people who have lived over the past years and even people today who have also been used by God in great ways. God is still doing great things through ordinary people who are surrendered to Him.

According to the world, I am just an ordinary person as well, *but* I know I have a *big God* who lives in and through me! I know that "EVERYTHING is possible for him who believes" (Mark 9:23). I don't ever want to limit God with doubt and unbelief, but rather with my faith give Him a body to live in and work through to do *unlimited things!* How I want to walk in the fullness of God's love and also the fullness of His power!

Many people seem to have the wrong idea and think that being a Christian is the most dull and boring thing to be. It is anything but that! It is the most exciting thing in the world! Think about it—to know the Living God personally and have Him actually live within you through His Holy Spirit! The old saying that the sky is the limit does not even hold true, for the sky is *not* the limit There are *no limits!*

I love the verse that Paul wrote:

> *I have become its servant by the commission God gave me to present to you the word of God in its fullness—the MYSTERY that has been kept hidden for ages and generations, but is now DISCLOSED TO THE SAINTS. To them God has chosen to make known among the Gentiles the GLORIOUS RICHES OF THIS MYSTERY—which is CHRIST IN YOU, THE HOPE OF GLORY!*
>
> Colossians 1:25-27

> *Christ in you and me, the hope of glory!*

Think about it. The word *hope* in this verse actually means "earnest expectation." *Glory* means "the presence and manifestation of God"! So what that verse is actually saying is:

> *Christ in us—the earnest expectation of the presence and manifestation of God!*

We can expect to *see* Christ's hands working through our hands, reaching out and touching people's lives, bringing healing and deliverance. We can expect to *hear* Him speaking through our mouths. We can expect to *feel* Him walking in our

feet, leading us where He wants us to go. We can expect to *see* all of His power, His love, His joy, His peace, His wisdom, etc., flowing through us—and everyone else will *see* Him too! I don't have to look out to find His strength, I just need to remember to look within. He is there!

God's Greatest Desire

God has referred to Himself by various names in the Bible that give us more of a glimpse of who He is. They show us His characteristics, what He does, and what He loves. They have been such a great help for us to get to know Him. We can see that God's heart is to reveal Himself more and more to His people. Some of the names which we find in the Bible are:

Jehovah Sabboath—The Lord of Hosts (1 Samuel 1:3)

Jehovah Hoseenu—The Lord our Maker (Psalm 95:6)

Jehovah Jireh—The Lord our Provider (Genesis 22:14)

Jehovah Rapha—I am the Lord that Healeth Thee (Exodus 15:26)

Jehovah Nissi—The Lord our Banner (Exodus 17:15)

Jehovah Mekaddishkem—The Lord our Sanctifier (Exodus 31:13)

Jehovah Tsidkenu—The Lord our Righteousness
   (Jeremiah 23:6)

Jehovah Shalom—The Lord our Peace (Judges 6:24)

Jehovah Rohi—The Lord our Shepherd (Psalm 23:1)

Jehovah Shammah—The Lord is There (Exodus 48:35)

Jesus—my Lord

As I thought about all of these names, I realized how God has been revealing Himself to His people more and more throughout the years. As generations have passed, He has given us a greater revelation of who He truly is. It is the will of God that we *know* Him.

As we approach the last days, God is revealing more and more of Himself to us—He is actually revealing His very *heart* to us! He not only wants us to know *about* Him, His characteristics, and what He is like, but He wants us to *know Him*. For this reason, He is pouring out the depths of His heart to us—to this generation! He wants us to *see* and *know* Him intimately. He wants each one of us to know His heart—His love that "surpasses knowledge"!

I have *heard* the heart of God saying....

"I love you!"
"I LOVE YOU!!"
"I LOVE YOU!!!"

I have *heard* the longing of God's heart crying out to His children....

"My love is *always* for you—
My heart is *always* calling you to Myself—
My desire is to *always* be close to you!"

I thought about that *picture* I described at the beginning of this book: the *picture* of God calling down to all of us, saying, "I love you, I love you, I love you," and yet nobody hearing Him or responding to those words of love. I thought about what God truly wanted to see and hear. How He would have *loved* to *see* everyone stop what they had been busy doing to listen to His words of love! How He would have *loved* to have everyone raise their arms to Him as a child reaches up to his or her father in love and adoration! How He would have *loved* to have everyone look up into His eyes and respond back by saying, "I love You, I LOVE You, I LOVE YOU!" How that would have touched God's heart!

As we grow to know His heart, I believe that we *will* respond to Him like that. As we grow to know His love, we *will* love Him back and we *will* want to live our lives to please Him out of that love for Him! God desperately wants each one of us to know His love.

So what is God's greatest desire? His greatest desire is to hear us say, "I love You!" to Him. God's greatest desire is for us to know His love—and to have us love Him back with all that we are—"with all of our heart, with all of our soul and with all of our mind" (Matthew 22:37).

God's greatest desire is our heart...
His greatest desire is *your* heart.

The Lord your God is with YOU,
He is mighty to save.
He will take great delight in YOU,
He will quiet YOU with His love,
He will rejoice over YOU with singing.
Zephaniah 3:17